I0714048

VII: (SEVEN)

WAR OF ROSES BOOK 2

LANA SKY

VII

VII: (Seven)

VII: (Seven) By Lana Sky

Copyright © 2019 by Lana Sky
All rights reserved.

No part of this publication may be reproduced, distributed, or transmitted in any form or by any means, including photocopying, recording, or other electronic or mechanical methods, without the prior written permission of the author.

This is a work of fiction. Names, characters, businesses, places, events and incidents are either the products of the author's imagination or used in a fictitious manner. Any resemblance to actual persons, living or dead, or actual events is purely coincidental.

ISBN: 978-1-956608-04-5

ACKNOWLEDGMENTS

Mickey, thank you so very much for taking the time to help me perfect this draft. As always, your feedback and expertise have been invaluable. Thank you, Charity for applying the final touches on this draft.

Thanks so much to everyone who supported this draft along the way, including the many beta readers who provided encouragement along the way! Please keep in mind that this story includes dark, graphic and explicit content matter that is not suitable for readers under the age of 18—or for readers who are uncomfortable with the following subject matter: explicit sex, mentions of sexual abuse, and graphic depictions of violence.

PREFACE

Shakespeare once posed the infamous question, *What is in a name?*

Everything, of course. Your soul. Your identity. Your fate.

It's why Robert feared his. That fancy, official moniker was a constant reminder of what his title as a Winthorp truly meant in the grand scheme: that he was nothing more than a pawn shoved across the game board by his own father.

Deep down, my husband thrived on the only aspect he ever had control over: terror. Like an artist, he cultivated it in other people and despised it in himself. He died of it.

In a suitable irony, so did his wife.

CHAPTER 1

How fitting is it that the old Ellen Winthorp meets her grisly end in a madman's lair, surrounded by scarlet? In a mocking array, the color paints the walls, accents, and every bit of furnishing. Red is all I see—like fire, consuming the remnants of my soul.

Curled on the floor, clutching my hand to my chest, I choke back a scream as the weight of my injury registers throughout my body. *Fire, pinching, aching, throbbing...* But, of all the emotions to feel...relief shouldn't be one of them.

"Ellen?"

A calloused palm grazes my cheek, jarring me from my thoughts. I blink, surprised to find my eyes are overflowing. The moisture blurs my vision, obscuring the figure crouched before me. Vanya.

"Let me see it," he commands. "Give me your hand!"

I can't silence a groan when he pries my arm from my side. Even the slightest touch triggers an avalanche of throbbing pain. Instinct warns me not to look down at the source: my left hand. Snippets of memory sneak into my thoughts anyway like a mocking slideshow. Blood. Bone. A sawing blade…

What the hell have I done?

"Jesus Christ!" Vanya recoils from me, his face pale. "Don't move!" He scrambles to his feet and returns a moment later, juggling an armful of supplies. Standing over me, he bites his lip, eyeing the puddle of blood spreading across the carpet. "Mischa… He didn't—"

"No." I shake my head. I'm not trying to spare Mischa further judgment, either. I need to hear it said out loud. "I… I did it to myself."

"Why? What the hell were you thinking?" He grits his teeth, but a relieved sigh robs his voice of any true anger. "Never mind. It doesn't matter. I need to stop the bleeding."

He sinks to his knees and presses a wad of cloth against my hand. I'm only vaguely aware of what he's really doing: staunching the bleeding from the grotesque stump where my ring finger used to reside.

A strangled laugh rips from me before I can help it. What a shame that Robert never gave me a ring—severing all ties to him would be a lot less dramatic in that case.

"Stay with me," Vanya warns, his voice gruff with concern. After a few seconds of pressure, he withdraws the bloodied cloth and wets it with liquid from a brown bottle. "I'll have to stitch it shut or it will continue to bleed. This will hurt like a son of a bitch."

I wince as he reapplies the cloth, but the physical pain is nothing compared to the chaos raging in my psyche. Twenty-three years of my soul have been sliced away without a second thought, and I don't know who's left behind—or what she wants.

Pain?

Torment?

Or, dare I even think…*Mischa*?

"Keep this covered," Vanya warns.

I glance down and find that he's wrapped my entire hand in gauze. Regardless, scarlet seeps through in vain.

"Damn it!" He fumbles to grab a small vial from his scattered supplies. "Here, hold on—" After priming a needle with the clear liquid from the vial, he injects it into my arm. The brief sting barely registers as a wave of dizziness washes over me, smothering the pain. "Now, stay here." Almost in afterthought, he mutters, "I need to find Mischa."

With that, he gathers his supplies and leaves.

Despite his warning, vanity wins out over exhaustion. I need to see…

Biting back a cry, I stand, holding my left arm awkwardly at my side. My knees feel like jelly and the room spins as I stagger to find my balance. In the end, I have to cling to the wall and make my way step by step into the bathroom. There, in the mirror, I find a stranger.

Her blue eyes are familiar. Briar? Ellen? Marnie? But no. Her cold, empty expression is the handiwork of only one creature. Mischa. He's claimed this new, untouched part of me. He's even given her a name.

Little Rose.

He doesn't let me sleep. The moment I drag my battered body to the mattress and attempt to lower my head, the door flies open and my tormentor invades. I open my eyes to track his predatory advance across the room. He's dressed in black now, a color-choice which just so happens to disguise any blood.

But at least he's whole. Both of his hands are intact, gesturing sharply as he speaks to someone behind him.

"…I went to him," he growls. "The asshole wouldn't dare attack me directly—"

"Oh?" another man interjects. Vanya? "Before last night, I would have believed so. Before I learned that you baited him. Toyed with him. And her? You let her think you killed—"

"Enough."

"Fine," Vanya concedes. He's changed his clothing and wiped the blood from his hands, but his haggard face betrays only exhaustion. "Play your game. But is *this* necessary?"

"*You're* the one who suggested I make her useful," Mischa snaps. Cocking his head toward Vanya, he adds, "So here's a chance for you *both* to prove your loyalty. Do the job without word of it getting back to Sergei."

"And her?"

"Get up," Mischa hisses, this time directing the words at me.

I flinch as his arm lashes out in my direction. Rather than a blow, something lands inches from my face. Square. Small. Plastic. My brain scrambles to identify it. A credit card?

"I have a job for you," he declares.

"J-Job?" I roll onto my side, biting back a groan. "What are you—"

"You're no longer my captive," he snaps, crossing his arms. "And with your husband dead, you're no use to the Winthorps either. So I suggest you choose your next steps wisely. Work with me or take your chances out there."

His words batter my exhausted brain. Deciphering them is like putting together a puzzle with jagged, razor-sharp pieces.

"So…then what am I?" I ask, my voice hoarse. "Why keep me?"

"Maybe you should ask how?" He raises an eyebrow. "How can you make yourself useful? Do what I fucking ask. Unless you think you can go crawling back to your precious Winthorps. With the son dead, maybe you can marry the father?"

I flinch. "So what do you want?"

"Go with Vanya," he says, jerking his chin in the other man's direction. "Buy a wardrobe fit to mourn your husband in. I'm tired of watching you sully my mother's clothes." He leaves, storming into the hallway.

"Don't worry about him." Sighing, Vanya comes to my side and hooks his hand beneath my shoulder, helping me to my feet. "Just move," he urges, guiding me forward. "I've got you."

The halls of the manor pass in a distorted blur. It's almost as if I blink and we're outside where the blazing sun reflects off a black van waiting at the foot of the steps. After fastening me inside the back seat, Vanya climbs in beside me.

"We've got at least an hour's drive," he says, casting a wary look at the manor behind us. "Get some sleep. Don't ask questions. You don't realize how lucky you are…"

But maybe I do. At least an hour, free from Mischa.

I couldn't have prayed for that much…but it's not a reprieve.

Time is just another weapon in his arsenal. Now I have longer to ponder what use he has for me now.

Because, without Robert, I'm useless to him.

And we both know it.

CHAPTER 2

"We're here."

Vanya shakes me awake, but it takes several slow blinks before my eyes focus well enough for me to regain my bearings. Narrow space. Enclosed. We're still in the van. Beyond the window, I make out a row of buildings. Their black awnings and brick façades stand out seemingly not one of the hotels or mysterious venues I'm used to being smuggled into.

"Just take it easy," Vanya warns as he maneuvers my arm around his shoulder to ease me from the van. "We'll make this quick, and then you can sleep on the way back."

Quick. My stomach lurches at the word. Was that twisted code for a more nefarious game?

After a few short paces, we enter the nearest building. Inside, clothing hangs from black velvet walls while a hostess mans a desk at the center of an elegant lobby. Beyond her is a waiting area with leather chaises. A store of some kind? It reminds me of the exclusive boutiques Briar frequents.

The people here must be used to patrons a bit more haggard than the polished circles my sister surrounds herself with, however. The girl who greets us doesn't bat an eyelash at my battered, bruised frame.

"We made an *appointment*," Vanya says.

"Of course." She nods and beckons us forward with a wave of her hand. "This way. Your men can bring the delivery around back."

Delivery. Her careful tone strikes a nerve. So Mischa planned this trip to mean more than a shopping spree. Of course he did.

I crane my neck and spot one of his men carrying something from the van out front. Before I can decipher what it is, Vanya tugs on my arm.

"Come." He guides me to one of the chaises at the center of the waiting area before he takes up a position near the mouth of the showroom. "Quick," he mouths.

But when the sales girl returns, I doubt speed is what she has in mind. Behind her, another woman pushes a rack filled with various items of clothing.

"We were told to select some items for you," the girl explains. Her name tag reads Jenny, and her smile is genuine enough. "However, we still like to get a feel for the style of our clients. Perhaps you'd prefer to select them yourself?"

Select. Style. Myself.

I don't think I've ever had clothing of my own. Always Briar's old things or hand-me-downs from the servants.

I don't even think I have a favorite fabric, or cut, or style.

Mischa had counted on that. Apparently, he had them just give me clothing "at random" without any thought put into what I might like. A part of me is exhausted enough to feed into the narrative of his prisoner and refuse to supply any input. It's what Vanya expects, and he eyes me with more concern than I'd like.

To be fair, I don't even know which of the garments hanging on the frames calls to me the most.

"You can show me," I hear myself croak. "I'd like to see what you have."

An hour later, Vanya finally intercedes, cutting the shopping trip short. With swift efficiency, he has the items I already selected brought out to the van before he comes for me himself and helps me to my feet.

I barely have enough time to choke out a parting thanks before we're back on the road and whatever drug he injected me with earlier takes its full effect. My tongue feels too heavy to control, and questions spill from it unbidden.

"Did I just help him commit another crime?" It's funny. I can't even come up with a solid tally of the criminal acts I've done for Mischa so far.

"Don't worry about it," Vanya replies. "You did nothing."

"He sold something," I decide, using what little logic I can muster as pain gnaws at my consciousness. "What?"

"Nothing. At least… *You* won't be the one forced to answer for it." He looks away, his jaw tight. "Just try to get some rest."

But I don't sleep on the way back. I die, am reborn, and awaken as something else. Someone else.

Someone whole despite her broken body. Her clothing and her life have been bought on a monster's dime—but she's more reckless than the old Ellen Winthorp ever was. Or maybe she's just that damn tired.

"Easy does it." Vanya's breath bastes my cheek, drawing me awake.

The world sways around me, but it's seconds before I realize why: I'm in his arms.

Gingerly, he carries me into the red room and sets me down on the bed. "Sleep."

Already numbed by the drug and pain, I don't resist unconsciousness as my identity continues to morph around me.

CHAPTER 3

"Get up."

I groan as awareness returns in agonizing snatches. Whatever drug Vanya gave me was of dangerous quality—the type of all-consuming drug the old Ellen Winthorp might have chased to numb the pain of her existence. For the first time in days, I didn't dream of a damn thing, and yet I awaken to an unfolding nightmare.

"I said get the hell up."

I blink my eyes open and find a demon with golden hair standing above me. He's still wearing black and his hair hangs loosely around his shoulders. "Get up!"

When I don't comply with his commands, something hard nudges my side. His boot?

A mattress conforms beneath me, but when I turn my head, the carpet is closer than it should be. Am I in another dungeon, or did he move me to a different room while I was asleep? But no…

The red walls are the same, as are the sheets. But the bed frame is gone, and so is the vanity, and the wardrobe, and any other sense of furnishing.

Like magic, he's turned the tables once more.

"From now on, if you want a fucking thing, you buy it your damn self," Mischa snarls, proving my suspicion correct: Somehow, he stripped the room bare. "Get dressed." He kicks the mattress, spurring me into a sitting position. "I have a job for you."

Unease coils in my belly. "A job." After swallowing hard, I add, "Being a mule for you to smuggle something into a boutique?"

His eyes widen. He didn't think I noticed?

"Or," I continue, "as a whore?"

With Robert gone, those are the only two uses he could have for me.

But his expression reveals nothing. Just bitter impatience that bristles as our gazes meet.

"Do not test me, Robert's—" He breaks off, scowling, but I can guess what word he held back. *Wife.* "Get. Dressed."

He didn't remove my new clothing, at least. The items are still packaged in boxes and bags piled behind him in one corner of the room. Cautiously, I stand and take a step, but my buckling legs nearly pitch me over.

"Easy," Mischa hisses. He grabs my arm, steadying me—but, surprisingly, I don't feel any pain. The drug must still be in my system.

"I'm fine." Taking care with my bandaged hand, I stagger toward the clothing and fish out the first outfit I can reach: a white dress.

I shed my filthy clothes and pull on the new dress over my head one-handed. When I try to smooth the hem, a drop of fresh blood seeps into the fabric. Spreads.

"I...I need to wash," I croak as my thumb rubs at the spot in vain.

He says nothing, but he doesn't stop me, either, when I turn toward the bathroom and limp over the threshold. Spotting my reflection in the mirror, I freeze, fixated by the mound of bandages around my left hand. It looks worse than I've imagined. A vibrant scarlet taints sections of the white gauze. Within seconds, it's dripping red, red, red.

Vanya left some supplies for me. I spot them arranged neatly on the counter, and perhaps it's delirium from blood loss that makes me sway, rather than gratitude. With my intact hand braced against the counter for leverage, I use my teeth to snag a piece of gauze from the bandage and unravel it layer by layer. There's no point in being brave. Not here. I moan and gasp at every tendril of burning pain that roils through my arm as more of the injury is exposed.

Reddened, inflamed flesh. A bloodied, gaping socket.

Oh God. I turn away, choking back bile as the gravity of what I've done sinks in. I've never hurt myself before. I never held a knife against my own flesh and contemplated the damage I could do.

But I remember it all now. Holding the blade, pressing down, tasting salt on the air... It took me three agonizing attempts to cut through the bone on my own. Then I vomited and dropped the knife. So someone else had to sever the last bit of muscle and tendon.

The same man who snatches my wrist now, preventing me from dripping more blood onto the floor. "Look at me," he growls. "Don't you dare pass out—*look at me!*"

Too exhausted to turn my head, I settle for watching him in the mirror's reflection. My blurred vision creates a twin for him, equally as cold as the original. Both hiss in disgust as my head lolls, too heavy to lift.

"Sit on the counter." He clears a space with a swipe of his hand, sending medicinal bottles and tools crashing to the floor. "*Sit on the fucking counter*—come here. No! Hold on to me, damn it!" Grunting, he grips my thigh and lifts me onto the counter's ledge himself.

"I...I'm going to faint," I admit against his shoulder. My head feels hot. I have to suck the air down into my lungs and hold it there before exhaling. In. Out. Slow. Slower.

Mischa says nothing. He muscles in closer, forcing my legs wider to make space for his bulk. Like a wall, his body pins me against the mirror. To keep me from falling, I realize. At the same time, he douses my hand in searing liquid and reapplies more gauze with much less tact and expertise than Vanya.

"You won't die," he mutters as if annoyed by that fact. "But it shouldn't keep bleeding with the stitches…" He steps back while I cling to the faucet with my good hand. "Don't move." In a ruthless motion, his gaze sweeps over me.

I copy him and choke on a gasp. So much for the new Ellen; my pretty white dress is ruined, painted red.

As I stare, Mischa snags the front of my dress in his fists and yanks, ripping the expensive material right down the middle. Before I can protest, he tosses the remains into a nearby trash can.

"You have five minutes to get changed, then meet me downstairs," he declares before storming from the room.

Five minutes. I waste three of them trying to remember how to stand on my own before I give up and crawl back to my stack of clothing. This time, I select a black dress. It's longer, made of wool, with long sleeves. With less than two minutes to spare, I stagger to the top of the stairs and find Mischa glaring up at me from the bottom of them.

I take my time, inching down each step, but he never moves to rush me along. Just as my foot hits the ground floor, he snatches my wrist and pulls me through the front door. The moon hangs above, adding a silvery glow to the harsh darkness that obscures most of our surroundings. I faintly make out three of his men lurking beyond the threshold. They follow us into a waiting van.

In a way that's beginning to feel routine, Mischa sandwiches me between himself and the door, all but daring me to test the lock on my own. Two of his men take the front and passenger's seats while the third lingers behind, openly sporting his weapon.

The driver must already know where to go. He takes off without any input from Mischa and the trip commences in tense, unbearable silence. Only a few hours ago, I would have maintained that silence.

Now, a question springs from my lips. I blame the drug. "Have you gone back on your threat? Will you kill me now? Or will you whore me—"

"Oh, but I *did* kill you," Mischa says. He doesn't bother to lower his voice in the presence of his men. His poisonous tone drips into their ears, infecting us all. "I killed the pathetic little bitch you used to be. And as I told you, whoever you are now…you work for me. Or can you not survive without that fucking mask you called Robert Winthorp?"

"Why?" I'm not talking about the violence or the money. "Why does it even matter what I do? Without Robert, I'm worth nothing to you—"

"Oh." He chuckles darkly, eyeing his scarred knuckles. "He wouldn't try to barter for you if you were worth *nothing*."

My mind goes blank. "R-Robert tried…to barter for me?"

He didn't mean to tell me. Irritation flickers across his expression like a ripple in a pond's otherwise calm surface.

"What did he offer?" I ask.

Rather than answer, he turns to gaze out his window. Everything down to his posture warns me to shut up. Back down. But as he said himself, the woman I once was is gone.

"Money?" I ask. "Land?"

His mouth grows tighter with every guess. I'm shooting in the dark.

"Tell me what he offered!"

"More than a million," he spits, grating the words through clenched teeth. "And don't you fucking think for a second that I won't still slit your goddamn throat—"

"What?" I jerk back against the stiff cushions of the seat. "You're lying."

Mischa raises an eyebrow. "Am I?"

My head hurts. I cradle it in my good hand, digging my fingertips into my aching temple. The harder I press, the more confused I feel.

"Then why not trade me? Or send my body to him?" A million. That amount sends a shiver down my spine. Robert was frivolous with money, but never like that. "Why—"

"This was never about *you*. You were always a worthless fucking token that fell onto the game board. And now?" He gives me a cold, soulless appraisal while stroking his chin. "I just want to see how long it takes me to break the little toy I stole."

The threat is almost convincing. Almost. But he's forgotten one thing: I grew up in this world as well and I am well-versed in the language of men and money.

"That doesn't make sense—"

"I suggest you shut your fucking mouth and carefully consider your remaining options," he warns. "I don't have much patience for either widows *or* wives—"

"Enough! You are not my husband."

He blinks. So do I. The grit in my tone shocks even me. "You…you are not Robert," I add. "I don't owe you a damn thing. If you want to kill me, kill me. I'll even do it myself…" I eye my mangled hand, horrified by my own boast. How easy would it be to cut a little lower and a lot deeper? "I'm not *your* captive anymore. So if you want me to work for you, then you earn my respect. My trust... This toy is not afraid of being broken."

I'm panting with the effort it took to get the words out. *Stupid.* Shutting my eyes, I press my skull back into the headrest. Do I regret what I've said? The answer terrifies me more than any rage Mischa could ignite.

No. I don't.

Not even as his breath scalds the tender flesh of my throat.

"And there she is," he growls. Is the grudging respect I hear a result of delirium? "The bitch without her mask. Can she back up the bullshit spewing from that pretty mouth?" He presses something against my palm and my brain shies from identifying it. Hard. Leather? "She better be able to."

He pulls away, and when I open my eyes, I find my hand wrapped around something thick. Long. Partly metal.

A knife.

A thrill runs through me as I tighten my grip on the handle. Am I its intended target—and he's just toying with me—or is the weapon meant to serve a more nefarious purpose?

Maybe as a reminder: *you've already sliced away part of yourself...*

Are you willing to sacrifice more?

You better be.

CHAPTER 4

"Hide it," Mischa commands, nodding to the blade. "Now."

It's too long to smuggle beneath the dress. Thinking fast, I lean forward and slip it handle-first into one of my new boots. Luckily, the blade is slim enough to avoid slicing into my skin, but the added weight is a chilling burden.

Sitting upright, I stare out the window and avidly study our surroundings. We're in the country, just beyond civilization, judging from the power lines that span the distance—but near a Winthorp stronghold if Robert was willing to trade for me. That detail should narrow down the potential areas, but in reality, I could be anywhere. The Winthorps owned property all over the world.

It was one of the many reasons I could never dream of leaving Robert.

He would always find me.

"We're here," the driver announces.

Here is…nowhere. We're parked on a dirt road that extends beside a thicket of trees. Only the glow from the headlights casts enough illumination to see by. From what I can tell, there isn't a building in sight.

In fact, it's the perfect place to bury a body.

I jump as Mischa muscles open the door on his end and takes my arm. "Come on."

He shoves me forward, toward a narrow expanse of naked field. An ominous shiver racks my spine as paranoid suspicions fester on my unease. Is this how he'll do it? Shoot me from behind?

"Hurry up!"

My hesitant, wooden steps are too slow. He gains on me in no time, drawing even with my shoulder.

From the corner of my eye, I see him manipulate an object held between his hands. A gun.

With deft motions, he removes the safety and cocks it. "You're afraid," he murmurs when I jump at the sharp noise. "Even better. You may not like to gamble, Little One, but you've been playing the wrong game. This is your biggest risk yet. You fuck up and we're both dead." His gaze warily sweeps the landscape, searching for anything that might raise alarm.

"Why trust me?" My nerves hum, awakened by his unease. I flex my fingers impatiently. Should I reach for the knife now? "In fact, isn't your war over now that Robert is—"

"Who said anything about trust?" Mischa wonders before I can decide on an answer to my dilemma. "No, this is about survival. Do you want to die as a worthless pawn, *Ellen*, or do you want to live?" He tucks the gun into the back pocket of his jeans and comes to a stop a few paces ahead of me. "Make your choice now."

He lifts his foot and slams the heel over a seemingly random spot in the ground. A spot that *moves*, breaking away from the rest of the earth to reveal a roughly dug hole. A wooden hatch covered it, blending in with the dirt in the dark. Beneath it, a man peers out, a pistol raised. My heart falters as the barrel drifts in my direction before settling squarely over Mischa.

"State your business."

"I have an appointment," Mischa retorts without a shred of concern given to the weapon. "Your boss is expecting me, and I'm short on time, so I suggest you take us to him before I give him advice on how to better train his dogs."

The vicious taunt goes unchallenged by the man. He merely nods toward the ground. "Leave your weapons here."

With a sigh, Mischa withdraws his gun and places it at his feet.

Unsatisfied, the man in the hatch turns to me. "Weapons."

"She's unarmed," Mischa says. His smug scoff portrays indignation I doubt even Robert could pull off: *As if I'd ever arm a bitch.* "She's my accountant. I already cleared her with your boss. Besides, if she *were* packing, the men you have lurking in the woods would have alerted you."

Mischa cuts his gaze to the swath of trees behind us. Only then do I make out flickering shadows among the underbrush. So we were being watched the entire time. If he knew, then why the blatant show of cocking his own weapon? Looking at him, I can't tell. His expression reveals nothing.

Sighing, the man in the hatch lowers himself deeper into the hole. "Come in."

Mischa starts forward, and I creep in his wake. Between his feet, a ladder descends into the hole. At the bottom of what appears to be at least a ten-foot drop, a faint glow betrays a larger space below. Turning to face me, Mischa descends the ladder first. When his head disappears below the earth, I follow, using my uninjured hand to feel for each rung.

"Watch it." Someone palms my waist when my heel strikes the bottom level: packed earth. Mischa.

I look at him, blinking as my eyes adjust to the surprisingly bright lights strung along a wire hanging along the top of a short tunnel. A few paces ahead, it opens onto a cavernous space cut right into the belly of the Earth. Wooden stakes reinforce the square structure, and near each corner stands a man hefting a large, semi-automatic weapon, like the ones carried by Mischa's men.

Seated on a metal folding chair is a balding man who's watching us approach, his arms crossed over his ample stomach. Surrounding him are several wooden crates. Only one has its lid removed, revealing the cargo it contains: black weapons packed into straw.

"Mischa," the man greets, his voice cold. "I have to admit that this is a surprise. I never thought I'd see the day when the pampered fucking prince would dare come crawling to me for lead. Who did you piss off this time? More Winthorps? Though I heard that the old man is gone. How's that for fucking irony? Done in by his own—"

"Anders," Mischa says over him, his tone equally cutting. "One would think that *you* weren't begging to sell your shit to *me*. Is this it?" He nods curtly toward the open box.

"It's pretty pricey for shit," Anders remarks. He cuts his gaze over to me before returning his attention to the man by my side. His disinterest makes one thing certain, and my sigh nearly barrels me over: I'm not one of the items for sale. "But you need the guns, or you wouldn't come to me. And," he adds with a hollow laugh. "You must have pissed off Sergei, or you would get your goods from him. Unless…" He rubs his dirt-covered fingers along his chin. "Unless you're trying to hide what you need the guns for. Ah, but concealing something from one of the ten heads. That would be against your fucking rules, wouldn't it?"

"Enough." Mischa's voice rings out through the room, ripe with authority. "The girl has the money. Name your price, and I'll take what you have now."

"My price?" Anders laughs darkly. "My *price*, Mischa, is way more than what you could offer for a few fucking guns."

"Oh?"

I taste the danger in Mischa's tone, even before his body jars mine, conveying a silent command. *Get ready.*

"And what would that be?"

"Your head," Anders says simply. The foreboding click of five guns cocking in unison bolsters the words. "It seems that the Winthorps have put a mighty big bounty on your head. From what I can tell, two have become one, and the remaining piece of shit wants you very, very badly, Prince."

Robert Sr.? It's almost funny how only now does it sink in, just what Robert's death means. His father will be on the warpath, and he will most certainly not want to rescue me. Mischa's lost his bargaining chip. Any benefit he might have gained from keeping me alive is surely good and gone now. So maybe he means it. A madman's curiosity is the only reason why I'm still breathing.

"So place your bets, Little Rose…"

My toes flex in my boots, dislodging the blade and coaxing it closer to the rim.

"Is that so?" Mischa says with a casual shrug. "By attacking me directly, I suppose you know what this means? You've just forsaken the protection of the *mafiya*."

"Now, tell me: What the hell do I need protection from a dead man for?" Anders chuckles, rising from his chair.

Slowly, he fishes a pistol from the waistband of his pants, but he doesn't bother to aim it. "All bets are off now. You wanted a war, Prince? You just bought yourself one—"

"You're right," Mischa says. "I have."

Boom!

Gunshots ring out as the world lurches, plunging everything into chaos. Dust flies. Darkness. Light. I'm choking on the thickened air, feeling for anything solid to cling to. I find it in the form of a muscular arm that flexes in recognition.

"Move!"

A chorus of pained groans almost drowns out the shout. More gunshots echo, but they sound too far away. Up above?

"Go!"

A hand rams against my back, shoving me forward. Up. Out.

Fresh air trickles into my lungs as someone manually hauls me out of the shaft and onto the field. Mischa. There's no time to get my bearings as he lunges forward, tugging me by my arm. I just run, giving in to his guidance. Eventually, we reach the trees where shouts echo, too chaotic to make sense of. Dirt and brambles nip at the bared skin of my legs and dislodge my boots. I'm clinging to Mischa more than I'd like—*clinging,* rather than letting him drag me along.

Suddenly, he comes to a stop, pushing me against a harsh surface. My heart stammers as my senses fight to identify it. Dry. Cold. Bark. A tree?

"Climb," he hisses.

I twist around to witness him peel his shirt off and tear it down the middle.

Cold, his gaze slices through mine. "Fucking climb!"

I reach for a low-hanging branch and attempt to use it for leverage to get off the ground. With only one functional hand, it's a pathetic attempt.

Behind me, Mischa scoffs. "Stay still." He seizes my waist and lifts, all but throwing me onto a narrow fork between two splayed branches.

Bark scrapes my palm as I scramble for purchase. "I'm slipping," I croak to him, fighting to keep my voice down. "I'm—"

"Don't panic," he warns from down below. "Wait for me."

With uncanny dexterity, he vaults into the space beside me and tugs my arm, righting my balance. His shoulders ripple as he manipulates the remains of his shirt. Twisting the fabric like a makeshift rope, he secures it around a higher branch and draws both ends taut. It holds just enough to help him climb to a higher ledge, and then another. He reaches down for me each way.

We're maybe twenty feet off the ground when he finally settles into a crook between two sturdy branches and pulls me up into the space beside him. It's precariously narrow. I straddle the thicker end of the branch, facing him, while he ties one end of his shirt around a higher branch and then twists the rest around his shoulder, securing himself to the tree.

"You'll fall from that end," he warns, flicking his gaze over my awkwardly splayed limbs. "Come here."

I make a show of scanning the ledge for a safer spot—but there's nowhere else to run. Below, footsteps crash through the forest and more shouts rise up. Something tells me they don't all belong to Mischa's men.

Yet, apart from panting with exertion, he doesn't seem too alarmed by our predicament.

"Unless you've slept in a tree before, I suggest you listen," he says as casually as if he were referring to the weather. "Come. Here."

Left with no other choice, I brace my hands along the branch for balance and inch my way toward him. I freeze when I'm close enough to sense the heat wafting from him like a furnace.

"Do you really think you can support yourself all night?" he asks.

A part of me wants to refuse and take my chances. But there's a dare lurking behind those dark eyes. One I know better than to ignore. *How far will you go for survival, Little Rose?*

"You went there unarmed?" I pose the question as I peel my good hand from the branch and brace it over his waist instead. A shiver runs through me at the contact. Gritting my teeth, I fight to disguise any reaction he could interpret as weakness and shift an inch closer. "Do you enjoy tempting fate?"

"Maybe I enjoy tempting *you*," he counters.

Up this close, there's no escape from his scent. It floods my head in dizzying waves: sweat, fresh air, blood. Most maddening of all, his pulse is racing beneath the calm exterior. Without being able to touch him, I might have been fooled. Rather than alarmed by the danger, he's *excited*.

"How?" I rasp, raising my voice as loud as I dare. "By nearly getting me killed—"

"I took a gamble," he explains, shifting to fully face me.

I look away, staring beyond his shoulder. From this angle, I have a direct view of the ground looming below. Fear is what makes my stomach clench—nothing else. Especially not him.

"Anders was a greedy little prick," Mischa continues near my ear. "One of the many men who underestimated me. Like your husband, he acted exactly how I predicted he would. And now…when the dust settles, I'll have his guns and no one will be able to do a damn thing about it."

A gamble?

"You knew he'd attack you," I deduce. "And yet you went there anyway."

"I knew that the benefits vastly outweighed the risks, Little One," he says. "That's your first lesson. Never risk what you aren't willing to lose."

Like his life? And mine.

"What about Sergei?" I ask. Anders mentioned him. Is this why Mischa did something so insane as meeting an arms dealer who wanted him dead? All to keep something from Sergei?

"Sergei…" Mischa sighs thoughtfully, his chest rising and lowering beneath my chin. "Sergei has his own goals in mind. They tend not to overlap with mine." His finger strokes my throat and I'm painfully aware of the necklace hanging from it. I can't stop myself from brushing the lump where the charm lurks beneath my collar. "But you wouldn't know anything about that. Would you?"

I grit my teeth. It's nearly impossible to tell if he's joking or if he knows.

And he's just toying with me.

"Don't think too much of yourself, Little Rose," he scolds, letting his hand fall. "Look at it this way: You are just a little pawn I'm not done playing with. But at least I'm honest in my intentions. In case you forget that, I suggest you remember that Sergei wants you only as a trophy—"

"Don't." I close my eyes as if to fend off the dark direction he seems determined to lead me down. Not again. "You've made your point."

"Have I?" Mischa wonders. He takes his unsecured hand from the bark of the tree and captures my chin with it, forcing me to meet his eyes directly. "You think I'm a monster," he says as if reading the word etched into my gaze. "I *am*. But I have always given you one thing that not even Sergei or your fucking husband ever would."

"Oh?" I somehow manage to copy his rasping tone, surprising myself with the ferocity. "And what is that?"

"A *choice*," he says. "Between being locked in a fucking cage or glimpsing what waits beyond it."

What a vicious, cruel lie. And he believes it. Though maybe it's true.

He gave me a choice between dying as Robert's wife or living as someone else—which puts him in possession of a dangerous weapon Robert Winthorp never utilized: power.

"So, what happens now?" I wonder, feeding off my latest dose of his hateful drug.

"We wait," he says, shrugging. "Vanya knows what to do. In the morning, my plan should come to fruition. When the dust settles, we return to Pecavi—"

"Pecavi?" I echo. I've heard that name before. "Is that the name of your house?"

Rather than supply an answer, he deliberately lets my question hang on the air. It seems I've found his own Sergei: the house is off-limits.

I let him draw his boundary and leave it be. But I don't sleep. I cling to my tormentor and listen to his heart beat as the forest sways around us.

And I never let my guard down.

CHAPTER 5

$\mathcal{M}$ischa finally guides me from the tree as a sliver of light begins to paint the horizon.

Disoriented and sore, I don't question him during the long trek through the woods. Finally, we return to that expanse of dirt road and find a van waiting with keys already in the ignition.

"Keep alert," Mischa tells me as he climbs behind the wheel. "Don't forget you have that knife."

After claiming the passenger's seat, I take his advice and scan our surroundings. Apart from scurrying creatures, I find nothing worth notice. Eventually, the motion of the van and the silence work to lull my brain into a false sense of monotony. The kind of dull idleness where dangerous thoughts take root.

My husband is dead. I feel a sudden urge to say it out loud, just once.

"He's dead." The words ring hollow, solidifying a thought that hurts to admit. I'd have to see it for myself. To truly know…

Robert owns me in a way that surpasses any other emotion I've lived by. I feel him in my bones. In my head. Death won't separate him from me so easily.

"How can I believe you?" I ask Mischa. Something he said keeps circling my skull. "How do you know it was really *Robert* who died? What about his father—"

"Tell me," Mischa says without taking his eyes off the road. "What reason would I have for lying about the *only* worth you had to me?"

He has a point.

"So, why keep me alive?"

This has to be the third time I've asked him as much in so many words. Why. Why. Why?

He has yet to give me a convincing answer.

"Should I kill you?" he wonders, turning the wheel to avoid a dip in the road.

For the first time, the landscape draws my attention. We aren't on our way back to his manor—unless he's taking a different route. We don't pass any of the landmarks I noted on our way here, and the fields grow more mountainous with every mile.

"Killing me would make sense," I reply, phrasing my answer carefully.

"Sense." He scoffs. "I don't deal in sense, Little Rose. I deal in what I can taste. Feel. Blood. Killing. Fucking. *You* can play with sense."

"So, fucking." My brow furrows as I parrot the coarse word. "Is that why?"

He looks at me sharply, forsaking the road. "Your cunt is nowhere near that good."

The vulgar terms set my cheeks on fire. "So, then—"

"Why?" he finishes for me. "How about I tell you *how*. How you can enjoy this gift of choice, Little One: You shut your goddamn mouth and you enjoy the ride."

"But why not let me go?" Testing him is a game I can't stop myself from playing. A gamble with brutal, unattainable dividends. I'll bankrupt my soul trying to win, but the few, rare lucky hands I've already won sate my nerve to try again.

"I may not be your husband, as you so kindly reminded me before," he says, "but make no mistake: I own you. You've seen too much. You can try to run if you want, but I will *find* you."

I swallow hard, sensing the threat resonate somewhere deep down in my belly. It's a promise.

"Though is dying with me any different from dying in Winthorp Manor?"

"Is it?" With Robert, I knew my place. I had a role and I performed it the best I knew how.

Here…

There are no rules, which upends my comfortable, if tiring, routine. Three days into my marriage with Robert and I had him pegged down to the minute as to how a typical encounter would begin and end. Twice as many days with Mischa and I still can't predict him from one second to the next.

As if to feed that narrative, he takes one of his hands off the wheel and swipes it along my cheek. "Since you seem so fond of ultimatums… Mention your husband again and I'll remember more stories about your mother and Sergei Vasilev." He presses his thumb over my lip, sealing the promise. "He's dead. From now on, you say only *one* man's name."

He doesn't identify just who that man is, but I have a sinking suspicion regardless.

"Do you understand, Little Rose?"

"Fair enough." I breathe the words against the window glass and watch them burst into puffs of fog. Just as quickly, they fade into nothing.

"Fair? I don't do fair. I calculate risk and I weigh my benefits."

And the benefits of keeping me alive? He doesn't reveal them, and maybe I prefer it that way. Few things could entice a man like Mischa. As a matter of fact, he's already named them: *"I deal in what I can taste. Feel. Blood. Killing. Fucking."*

One item can already be checked off that list, leaving just two…

Blood and killing.

CHAPTER 6

*D*espite what feels like hours on the road, the only semblance of civilization we come across is a small gas station consisting of two pumps and a tiny storefront. Faded advertisements obscure the windows, and there are no other patrons—or anyone, in fact—for what seems like miles.

Just empty, barren land.

Surprisingly, Mischa pulls into the lot and circles around to the building's rear end. There, my suspicion is proven false: A lone man is waiting, guarding a battered door. Dangling from his hip, in plain sight, is a gun. Alarmed, I look over at Mischa, but a faint smile shapes his lips and I bite back my warning.

"Stay here." He climbs out of the van, taking the keys with him. Together, he and the man enter the building and exit it moments later with something slung between them—a wooden crate.

In their wake follows a third man, hefting another intimidating weapon. They pack the crate into the van, and then Mischa forces me into the back seat. His two men occupy the front, and the driver takes off without a word of direction.

Ignored, I endure the silence as the daylight progressively fades. Eventually, the sound of a door opening jostles me back to awareness.

"We're here."

I blink my eyes open and find Mischa waiting for me outside the van. Behind him looms that impenetrable manor bathed in shadow.

I follow him silently, keeping as much distance as I dare. Inside, Vanya is standing near the foot of the stairs, his arms crossed.

"What did I say?" Mischa says to him. "There is *always* another method."

He must be alluding to a past argument, because Vanya sighs in exasperation and nods. "Yes, yes. But sometimes it's better to use caution—"

"Caution? Such as letting your brother continue to pull my strings?" When Vanya says nothing in response, Mischa chuckles. "It was a joke, Ivan. Did you handle things on your end?"

"Of course." Vanya shifts to reveal something I didn't notice in his hand: the handle of a gray duffle. He lets it fall to the floor and kicks it open to reveal the contents.

I can't stop my eyes from widening at the sight.

Money. Stacks of it.

"Good." Mischa crouches to rifle through the bills. He grabs a rubber-banded stack at random and then shoves the amount toward me. "Your cut," he explains as I gape at the offering. "Welcome to your new family, Ellen Winthorp."

When I don't reach for the money, he grabs my wrist and presses the bills against my palm until I have no choice but to accept them.

"We don't give a shit about blood here. This"—he nods to my hand—"is the only life we value."

With that, he snatches up the handle of the duffle and carries it across the hall. This time, I know better than to follow him.

"Be careful." Vanya's watching me, his expression thoughtful. After a tense second, he nods to the stairs behind him. "Go get some sleep."

"Goodnight."

I slip past him, entering the room beside Mischa's a few minutes later. It's still bare, devoid of anything but a mattress. Ignoring the sight, I switch on the light and rip the rubber band off the stack of dollars.

Sinking to my knees, I count them, peeling the bills apart with my good hand. Slowly. Precisely.

My price for joining Mischa's "family" is a hefty one, in the end. More money than I could ever dream of owning. More than Robert ever let me handle at one time. More than any man should ever give a "worthless whore."

Unless, of course…

He placed an even bigger bet on her life.

I'm still running my fingers through the loose bills when the door opens and Vanya enters. Facing me, he braces his back against the wall and nods to the money.

"Keep it safe," he warns. "The men won't dare steal from Mischa, but you…are not him."

"Thank you," I croak, my voice thick.

"Don't." He shrugs the gratitude off, squaring his jaw. "I'll get you something to put it in. Keep it on you always—"

"Why are you so nice to me?" I don't mean to come off as rude. Perhaps desperate? Mischa, as brutal as he is, speaks a language I can understand. But kindness? That is a foreign commodity in my world, and if Robert taught me one thing, it was that nothing came for free.

"Why?" Vanya looks beyond me, his mouth twisted thoughtfully. Finally, he sighs. "I would hope that, in her final days, someone would have shown some kindness to my daughter."

I cringe at the barely concealed pain in his voice.

A good woman wouldn't probe it.

"I saw her," I admit. Like a coward, I stare at the floor rather than meet his gaze. "At Winthorp Manor when she was held captive. Did Mischa tell you?"

"Yes."

I lift my head and meet his gaze, but he stares back unflinchingly, hiding nothing.

"He told me. And in her name, I want you to know that you have nothing to fear from me. However, I do have something I want to ask you, if that is all right."

"Anything." I can't help how eager I sound. "Please ask."

"You grew up there? In that place?"

I force myself to nod. "Yes."

"And your parents?"

Alarm dances down my spine. "Dead."

"And…your mother?"

My lips part just as Mischa's words come back to haunt me: *"If Vanya asks about her. Lie. Trust me on this."* The concept should be laughable. Trusting Mischa over the only man to show me kindness here.

But…

My new tormentor may be many things, but I'm not sure if a liar is one of them.

"Her name was…Martha," I lie. "She was a maid on the Winthorp estate."

"A maid?" He raises an eyebrow. "It's just that you remind me of someone."

"Oh?" My heart lurches in my chest. "W-who?"

"Someone," he repeats, staring past me. His mouth sags into a wry frown, but not even a second later, he shakes his head, banishing the expression. "Get some sleep. I'll get you something for the money in the morning."

He's gone a heartbeat later, closing the door behind him.

When heavy footsteps near the room, I assume it's him, returning for one last word. But no. Another man throws the door open, looming in the doorway.

"I gave you your payment," Mischa tells me, his voice rough. He found a new shirt from somewhere, though he wears the same filthy pants. "That is how it will be from now on. A transaction. You prove your worth—"

"Like by being a mule for whatever illegal things you sell?"

"Ah." He raises an eyebrow, his mouth quirked. "I gave you your cut, didn't I?"

I eye the money, flexing my fingers. "As if that makes it any better—"

"Don't lie." He advances a step closer. "You fucking like having it—payment. But since I've given you yours… I'm here to take mine."

I glance at him sharply. "And what is that?"

"Hmm…" He strokes his thumb along the bottom of his chin.

My heart races with every second he stalls. Anger is unnerving in him, but so is this: calculated thought.

"An answer," he finally says. "Was it really you?" When he glances at my bandaged hand, I know what he means. Was I the one controlling the knife? "Or will you play the victim? Claim you had no choice—"

"*I* did it," I hiss, drawing my bandaged hand to my chest. "Does that make you happy? The fact that I mutilated myself?"

His eyes narrow. I've caught him off guard. "Not mutilated," he insists softly. "I'm after your honesty, Little Rose. The one thing I fucking know for a fact he didn't teach you."

"And now he's dead." Spit flies from my lips, laced with vitriol. "So you can stop comparing yourself to him. Robert—"

"No." Anger resonates in his voice like a slap. "Have you forgotten so soon? Take a good look."

He sheds his gray shirt, tossing it into a ball on the floor. His arms flex in its absence, displaying every muscle rippling with tension. "I told you that you are only allowed to utter one man's name. Shall I teach you how to say it?"

The coldness in his gaze is such a stark contrast to the beautiful collage of scars and tattoos unfolding across his ribcage. My breath catches as my nerves spark, aware of his nearness.

"Mischa Mikhailovich Stepanov." He takes another deliberate step as I watch. Then another. When he's close enough, he cradles my chin against his fingertips, grazing my skin with the tips of his nails. "Now…I want to hear how it sounds when you scream it."

He shoves me back and works on the waistband of his pants with slow, deliberate motions. Anticipation ricochets through my veins, rendering me paralyzed as my heart picks up speed.

"I-I…I'm not your captive anymore," I gasp out. Though am I speaking to him? Or myself? "I—"

"I don't really give a damn what you are," Mischa says. He sinks to his knees over the end of the mattress, grasping my thighs in each hand. Then he waits as if he's expecting me to run. When I don't, he parts them slowly, watching my face with every inch of space revealed. "All I want is what I'm owed."

"Get off of me—"

Stealing my breath, his fingers slip beneath my dress and find me quivering—even as I try to bat his hand away. I'm slick. Ready. It's impossible to hide the truth from his touch. With him inside me, there is no escape.

"I knew it." His eyes flash as he swipes his thumb along my entrance and my body quakes in response. It's like each nerve short-circuits, rewired by every brutal caress. "*This* is how a woman speaks to the man she needs. You can't lie to me like this. You can't pretend…so don't. You've never ached like this for him."

I gasp out, squeezing my eyes shut against his heated expression: clenched jaw, heavy-lidded eyes. My inner muscles spasm, grasping greedily at his fingers. He's right. We speak our own language, and he's drowning me in nonsense.

"So, what will it be, Little One?" he wonders as he rocks his erection against my entrance, teasing me with the unbearable fullness. "Hard or slow?"

I writhe against the bed. Avoiding him…drawn to him. A pathetic whimper bubbles in my throat.

"Both?" Mischa murmurs into my ear. "As you wish. But first…" His fingers sink into my hair again, tugging. "I demand my payment in full."

He gives me no warning before he stretches me open with one thrust, pushing the air from my lungs and every thought from my head. My hips arch, driving him deeper even as I turn my face into the sheets, desperate to shut him out.

But he won't be erased so easily. His teeth nip at my earlobe, insistent and unforgiving. "Look at me. *Fuck*—look at me."

I open my eyes and cry out at the monster I find staring back. His eyes are aglow with unholy fire, his lips drawn back to bare his teeth. He grunts as he fucks me. Takes me. Breaks me.

There are no rules. Just chaos and the violent tempest that drives him in and out. Harder. Deeper. *Too much.*

"Give it to me, Little One," he demands, clawing at my hips for enough leverage to change the angle of his thrusts. It's like his aim is to bore through me. Into my soul. Into my head. "Give it to me."

My lips flutter and then fly apart as broken noise tears from my throat. "M-Mischa."

My cheeks heat with shame. I've lost this game. Or have I?

The sound of his name makes him rear up on his knees, his head thrown back, a groan building in his throat. Like a growl. Like thunder. Hungrily, his fingers bite into my flesh, claiming, grasping. "Say it again."

It's not the triumphant command of a conquer. It's...a plea?

"Shit... Say it again." Corded muscles strain against his flesh, distorting his outline. He's more beast than man, howling for release. "Fuck, say it—"

"Mischa."

His name holds its own power. Too fucking much for my head to contain. He bucks at the sound of it, hunching forward to sink his teeth into my shoulder so hard that I see white.

My lips part, but rather than a cry, something else slips from them, broken and bleating. "Mischa…"

The word ends on a moan as he flips me over, pressing my face into the sheets. With my body prone, he enters me from behind. His hips slam into me, and I take him as deep as I can—then even further than that. I taste him. I'm consumed by him. He beats his ownership into my battered flesh and rakes his name into my skin with his teeth.

I lose track of how long it lasts. How brutal he becomes. Bruising. Punishing.

Thoughtless.

Reckless.

Boneless.

I'm a mass of exposed nerves when he finally groans into my ear, flooding me with his release, but he never moves. I'm crushed beneath his weight, too exhausted to resist the unbearable pressure. A part of me considers lying there, letting his bulk drive every ounce of air from my lungs until there's nothing left. I could die like this.

"Hey." As he finally rolls onto his side, stars dance across my vision. "Look at me."

He's frowning when I do. With one hand, he reaches out to flick the sweat-soaked hair from my face. Whatever he finds makes him scoff in disgust.

"Still there," he declares, rolling onto his back. "Tell me, Little Rose. What would it take to drive him out of your skull for good?"

Robert? It's a comical question, though he doesn't seem to see it that way. His voice is gruff. Stern. Serious.

"Twenty-three years," I reply, alarmed by how dead I sound. How tired.

"What a shame," Mischa muses. "I don't have that kind of time." He shifts, turning his back to me.

I wait, but he doesn't stand yet. His heat prickles my skin, a foreign sensation. Robert never extended his presence beyond this point. Only now can I entertain the small possibility that it might have been some shred of mercy on his part.

After all, he never wanted to ruin me, break me, destroy me…

He just wanted to own me. I still wear his shackles, and I'm at a loss as to how to find the key—or if one even exists. What would it take to drive him out of my skull for good?

"He kept me blind."

Mischa stiffens at the sound of my voice, but I'm more shocked than he should be. I'm not used to speaking like this. Freely. Unease mingles with the breathless aftermath of the sex, churning my thoughts into a senseless mass that makes it hard to discern what's smart and what is…not.

"He never told me anything," I add. "And he used my ignorance as a cage."

There's so much I don't know about the Winthorps, or my mother, or the *Mafiya*. So much I'm not sure I ever want to learn.

"If you want to erase him, then…" The words linger on the tip of my tongue, too stupid to utter out loud. Too reckless. I'm tempted to swallow them down.

But no. I've already piqued the monster's interest. One taste of my bleeding soul and he wants more.

"What?" He's harsh, impatient. Curious?

I raise my gaze, hunting for his body through the dark. He's faced me again without my realizing it, meeting my probing stare with a brutal scowl of his own.

"Name your price, Little Rose."

Perhaps he's not far off. Maybe my cage never required a key. Just a price some mercenary would pay to buy his way in.

"Open my eyes," I say simply. "Let me learn this world for myself and tell me everything. Everything he never did."

CHAPTER 7

I don't dream…

But I know I'm in one before the cruel curtain is ripped away. I'm too happy. Too content. The warm body in my arms conforms to mine like no one ever has. So perfect…

I blink to make the scene clearer—to see his face just one last time.

I call for him…

But *then* reality returns and I wake up to a cruel world that looks the same as it always has: distorted snippets seen through the bars of the cage. It seems my current captor needs more convincing to release his pet bird from her prison. He wants me to ask him twice.

He wants me to beg.

One wouldn't know just from looking at him, however. He's still sprawled on his side of the bed, facing away from me as light streaks his back. But it's surprisingly easy to sense which directions his thoughts take in this moment.

Wherever a sane man's mind would venture, his travels the opposite path. Almost as if he likes to spite that tiny bit of humanity inside himself that only Vanya seems to think still exists.

"Little Rose…" He inhales deeply, as if sensing my attention, causing the muscles along his spine to ripple. "Did I say you could move?" He sounds half asleep.

But I'm not fooled. This creature, man or monster he may be, doesn't sleep. He watches me during the night. He studies me.

He still is.

Aware of his scrutiny, I lie back down, staring up at the ceiling. Whatever drug Vanya gave me all those hours ago has finally worn off.

It. Hurts.

Everything.

My hand is just another agony adding to the symphony of it blaring beneath my skin. My head aches. Back aches. My soul…

It's the most battered by Mischa's violent whims. He manhandles it even now as he makes me listen to every lazy breath he takes while I wait for his command to rise.

Seconds pass. Minutes. My reprieve never comes.

"You don't like being touched." He makes that claim while a shadow creeps toward my side of the bed, cast by his hand. A heartbeat later, he boldly strokes my hip. "Oh, I don't mean in *this* way."

As I shudder beneath his touch, his breath bastes the base of my throat, igniting sweat gathering there. In an instant, I'm ablaze.

"You don't mind the fucking. You tolerate it. It's the nearness you don't like. Contact." His hand stills as he comes to a sudden realization. "He never slept in your bed."

I say nothing, distracted by the sensation of his callused palm. Too heavy. Too warm. Too real.

"I will not show you the same mercy, Little Rose."

He tugs on my hip, yanking my body onto his torso. I'm now facing him directly, our bare flesh meeting with a wet slap. His eyes are heavy-lidded but stern, contradicting the slow, lazy smile shaping his lips.

"You will *breathe* me." His coarse tone transforms the words into the most dangerous threat: a shackle of promises. "There will be no escape. No reprieve. Whether you are awake, or asleep, or in my bed, you will never know any reality that doesn't include me."

His promise festers like poison in my stomach, eating through what little resolve I have left. I survived Robert, a badge I wear with pride. And yet...

Mischa is a whole new creature. One who's adapted to hone every weapon my husband never bothered to use. As if to feed that fear, his hands caress my shoulders, raising goosebumps with every bit of flesh they claim.

"Don't look so alarmed, Little Rose." He brushes his mouth against my cheek. "I think I've changed my mind. I *will* do this slowly. I might have twenty-three years to break you after all. In the meantime…"

He shoves me off and rolls effortlessly into a sitting position. With his back to me, the scars there stand out in stark contrast, catching the light.

"You want to be enlightened?" He stands and fishes his clothing from the floor. Once dressed, he looks at me from over his shoulder. "Then come and open your fucking eyes."

I rise obediently and stagger toward my pile of clothing. At first, I intend to grab whatever I can reach. He beats me to them, kicking a bag over so that its contents spill out for his inspection. One by one, he nudges the expensive fabrics with his bare toes.

"The black," he grunts finally. "Wear that."

I eye his selection and bite my lip: a thin dress with spaghetti straps.

"Why?"

"Why?" The smirk he's wearing alarms me more than his raw anger. "You're not with him anymore. So don't fucking dress like it."

"What do you mean?" Exasperation taints my tone. So many rules. *Don't do this. Don't think that. Don't wear those.*

My entire being must remind him of Robert. But how much of my identity is my husband and how much is just me? I'm terrified to realize that I don't know the answer.

"Why can't I wear this?" I point to a shirt in a delicate shade of pink.

He scoffs and snatches the garment from the floor. Then he rips it in half and tosses the torn pieces at my feet. "Because you aren't a fucking Winthorp doll in their pretty glass house."

He moves quickly, drawing a gasp from my lips before I even process why: He gripped my chin with one massive hand, tilting it roughly so that he can view me from a different angle. I'm not sure what he sees from his vantage point. Fear? Submission?

Or a challenge?

"Unfold your arms."

Alarm jolts through me, locking the limbs to my sides. "W-why?"

"Your arms." He snatches my wrists himself and wrenches them apart. His eyes rake over my exposed torso without mercy, but I don't miss how his tongue flicks along his lower lip with every inch gained. "I want you to think," he demands. "You listen to your body. Tell me how it wants to be dressed—not with fucking pink. Not like Briar.

Like…" Chuckling low in his throat, he leans in closer, and I assume he's relishing the involuntary swallow racking my throat. "You. How does little Rose want to be dressed?"

"Not like your doll." My fingers shake slightly as I test his grip, and I'm surprised when he lets me go. Slipping past him, I snatch another shirt from my pile on the floor. It's a light shade of blue.

Mischa says nothing as I pull it on and then shimmy into a pair of jeans. When I gather the nerve to face him, he's already near the door.

"Come." He jerks his chin and enters the hall. Daylight streams in from a nearby row of windows, ghosting over the ornate wall fixtures and painting a stark contrast to my barren room. Enlighten me, he said?

Perhaps he'll start with this.

"Do you own this place?"

Another raspy laugh rumbles from his chest—but this time, it lacks any humor. He sounds more guarded than anything. When we reach the staircase without him responding, I assume he won't play this game after all.

"Tell me," he says as he descends the first few steps, proving me wrong. "If I did, would that impress you?"

His back is to me, meaning he can't see how my mouth twists in genuine contemplation. Would it? The answer comes quickly. No. Robert possessed wealth in spades. Yet, underneath, he was a simple man who craved simple, base things.

"Of course not," Mischa assumes, answering for me. "You grew up in fucking Winthorp Manor. I'm sure your husband bathed you in diamonds."

Ironically, he's not far off. Though none of Robert's many gifts were truly mine. I had nice dresses that he kept locked in a closet, allowed to be worn only at his discretion. I had trinkets and baubles that were his taste, not mine. Even my own servants deferred to him always.

"You don't give a fuck if I own this," Mischa declares, gesturing to our surroundings with a wave of his hand. We've reached the lower level, and he leads me past the main entrance and down a hallway. "A better question is how. Go on. Ask it. I know you want to."

"Robert made his money through investments," I say, parroting a term I've heard flung around my entire life to explain away the wealth of the Winthorps. Investments. With money. Into something. The details were never explained.

"You know that's a fucking lie." Mischa doesn't waste putting any effort into the assertion. "The Winthorps trade in *flesh*, Little One. Women. Girls. They hide their business well, using a shipping company as a front, but it is slavery nonetheless."

"Y-you're lying," I rasp automatically. Robert was a lot of things, but a sex trafficker?

"Don't sound so surprised." Mischa shoots me a glance over his shoulder. For once, his smug grin is absent. "I'm sure you've suspected as much. What other 'investment' could amass a man enough money to buy the whole fucking world?"

"Maybe I was that naïve," I croak. So many things take on a darker connotation now. The foreign maids who staffed the manor. The secrecy around Robert's accounts. My heart pangs as I consider the unthinkable: Could I have played a role in it all unknowingly?

"So you didn't know." He sounds doubtful, even as the words leave his mouth.

"And you?" I wonder, eyeing his back. I've seen the scars that mark his body, but what horrors might lurk on his soul? "Do you trade in 'flesh' as well?"

The way he stiffens makes me second-guess that suspicion. His shoulders tense, almost as if he doesn't even recognize his own disgust.

"My family has always been less complex than your elegant Winthorps," he calls from paces ahead, continuing to walk without me. "We trade in simpler things: drugs, and guns, and money."

I force myself to keep moving, chasing him down a narrow corridor and into the dining room. When he takes a seat at the head of the grand table, I maintain the distance between us, staying near the wall.

"No slaves?" I don't mean to sound mocking.

"Oh, don't tell me, Little Rose." Mischa cocks an eyebrow. "You're *still* not impressed. Maybe I've pegged you wrong? You more than knew of his business. Maybe you got off on the thrill of it? Being the one woman he chose to keep?"

"The one?" I echo, my brow furrowing. "What makes you think I was his only woman?"

I expect him to sneer at the statement. Not frown.

"You *were*," he insists. "He may have fucked his whores on the side. I don't doubt that. But *you* were the one. The one he claimed. The one he needed."

It's almost too twisted to consider. "Needed?"

He laughs. Then he scowls. "To keep him sane."

A chill runs down my spine. God, it's like I'm hearing Robert again, hissing his insanity into my ear. *I need you, Elle.*

"Did he tell you that?" I rasp hoarsely. "Did you talk to him? Before—"

"No." Mischa shakes his head. "He didn't have to tell me a damn thing, Little Rose. I just know how pathetic men like him operate. How they crave a woman's devotion. Especially someone like you, pathetic and weak. If such a creature could still see the good in them, they can justify their fucking madness. *You* helped him sleep at night—"

"Don't blame me for what he was." I don't realize I've spoken out loud until he chuckles, eyeing me with amusement.

"Why not? You said it yourself: He never forced you. You chose to marry him. You chose to fuck him every night. You *chose* to give him your devotion. Don't lie to me and say you don't believe for a second that having you in his bed made it easier for him to do the twisted shit you know in your soul he's capable of?"

Maybe it did.

"But what about you?" I say, turning the tables the only way I know how: comparing them. "If your logic holds, then where is your woman? Your excuse?"

"She's dead." His mocking smile falls flat. "And I don't need anyone to fucking justify my actions." He shoves back from the table and advances on me too quickly to outrun. When he's paces away, he cradles my cheek with alarming gentleness, contrasting the anger smoldering in his expression. "You can try your little tricks on me, Little Rose," he taunts, stroking my jaw. "But I don't believe salvation can be found in your cunt."

"S-stop it!" My cheeks flame. "You have a strange idea of love."

His concept of the emotion is much more potent than mine. To me, love is duty. Sacrifice. But he makes it sound alluring. Dangerous. Capable of shaping men, and even more fantastical: changing them.

"And you don't?" Frowning, he draws his hand away. I think I've confused him. "Don't tell me… You never believed your fucking Winthorp was a white knight, capable of saving your soul?"

"Of course not." I force a laugh for good measure. He's mocking me. He has to be.

"You're serious." A shadow falls over his face. "That poor fuck. He thought you were. His wife. His love. He would have fucking begged for you—"

"But now he's dead," I interject, my throat tight. "And you? Did you beg for your love?" I don't know where the question came from—or why I'm so curious as to the answer.

Alarm runs down my spine as his eyes narrow.

"I didn't," he says in a soft, lethal tone. "Because I was a stupid fucking fool. I traded her life for another's. And you want to know something, Little Rose?" His fingers come to trace the hollow of my throat, catching me off guard. "That person wasn't fucking worthy."

I recoil and race to the other end of the room, desperate to put distance between us. Anna-Natalia, Vanya's daughter. He's talking about her. Traded her life, he said? I have a sinking suspicion whose life he traded it for.

Mine.

"Don't blame me for what you are, either," I hiss at the wall —but it's more of a plea than a rebuttal. Robert's already tainted my soul. I can't take any more.

More guilt.

More pain

More envy?

"Oh no you don't." Laughing, Mischa moves to stand opposite me, refusing to be ignored. "Look at me."

A sliver of blond hair obscures his gaze. Only the stern set of his mouth gives me a clue as to what he's feeling.

"You want me to enlighten you?" he asks. "Teach you what he never did? Let's start with the truth: All I want from you is the one thing you never gave him." He waits, ensuring he has my full attention. Then he smiles, displaying a terrifying array of white teeth. "I want your honesty, Little Rose. Can you give me that?"

He doesn't seem to really want an answer. Not now anyway.

"Let's start with your first lesson," he says, abruptly changing the subject. "Sit." He nods to the chair nearest him.

Heart in my throat, I approach it. This close, I'm aware of his scrutiny, how he eyes my quivering throat and heaving chest.

"Twenty-four years ago, the Winthorps started a war." He leans back against the wall, crossing his arms over his chest. Apparently, this story will be a long one. "Can you tell me why?"

I grit my teeth. My ignorance is a toy he constantly loves to play with. "You know I don't—"

"But you should." His tone softens, unnervingly quiet. "Because your mother was at the start of it."

I blink, unsure if he's joking—but there is no mocking smile to temper the impact of his words.

"Oh, don't look so shocked." He leans in and drags his thumb along my cheek as if savoring how my eyes widen. As I gape, he brings the digit to his mouth and flicks his tongue over it. Then he says, "I think you've suspected it all along, haven't you? That she was the very first. Marnie Winthorp. She was fated to be number one."

I clutch the surface of the table if only to keep from reaching for the necklace hidden beneath my shirt. I know he can see it: the desperation to know more that I can't even begin to suppress. I picture her. Marnie, beautiful Marnie. Not only was she a victim in the feud, but a cause of it? "How?"

"It's not what you're thinking," Mischa scolds. "It wasn't some petty, romantic squabble. Your mother was meant to pay a price, Little One. A life for a life."

"Then how was she the first?"

I expect him to elaborate, but he doesn't. Instead, he extends the silence, reminding me of Robert when he hunted, patiently anticipating the moment his chosen prey would take his bait.

So I bite. "Tell me!"

"Fine. Your Winthorps weren't always so high and mighty," Mischa counters. "Years ago, they had an arrangement with the *mafiya*. They ran our accounts, and we protected their interests."

His subtle inflection betrays what he really means: that his people were the muscle for Robert Sr.

"But your husband's father got greedy. He thought he could betray us, his allies. Your mother was meant to be his punishment. When she was taken, I'm sure they thought she was dead. So they retaliated."

With him and his mother? I don't dare ask. Instead, I remember something else he told me once. Anna-Natalia was number twelve. Was Briar meant to be thirteen?

"You said you traded one life for another," I say cautiously. From his expression, I can't anticipate his reaction. I have no choice but to forge on. "Mine? Briar's? For Anna—"

"*You* were never a damn factor in any of this," he says, reminding me of my fate: a decoy. How ironic that in both my encounters with him, I was always standing in for someone else. "It was always about Briar."

But he's lying.

"So then why didn't you go after her? In the woods," I say. "Don't lie to me by claiming it never happened. I know what I saw."

It wasn't a vivid dream after all. Briar was in those woods— and once again, he saved *me*.

Something flits across his gaze too quickly to name. "I miscalculated," he says finally and I flinch, caught off guard by the truth. "I thought that you might mean more to him."

"Either way, you killed him."

"But if I didn't?"

My stomach drops as Mischa turns from me, his voice a thoughtful murmur.

"If he lived. Would that make you turn against him, your precious husband? Knowing that he would have let you die as a sacrifice?"

"No." I'm as surprised by the admission as he seems to be. He whips around, eyeing me with predatory focus. "If Robert chose his sister over me...it would have been him being selfless."

Briar didn't carry his secrets. She couldn't warm his bed.

She never carried his seed.

"Selfless?" Mischa's thumb grazes my cheek and I jump. He's frowning again. Confused? "To let you die for him?"

"No." I shrug him off. "Because he would have finally let me go—"

"Mischa?"

We both turn to the doorway and find Vanya standing there.

Warily, his gaze darts between the two of us. "Your…input is needed," he says, wording the phrase carefully.

To hide something, I suspect.

From me.

"You can speak freely, Ivan," Mischa says. He passes me and enters the hall with his mentor on his heels. "It's not like Little Rose has a family to run to, should she escape."

I grit my teeth against a reply. Instead, I stand and pad after him, straining my ears for more. Maybe there's a reason Robert never enlightened me more than he needed to. Knowledge is addicting. It's power. Already, I'm seeing slight nuances in a different light.

Everything seems clearer, and maybe, deep down, I'm… relieved? Briar thought Robert would trade her for me. Is that why she used me as her own decoy? In the end, he proved her wrong.

And she finally won the only game that mattered.

"There was a complication," Vanya says, drawing my attention back to him. He and Mischa are paces ahead, navigating a section of the house I don't recognize. It's darker, the walls plainer and less ornate. Somewhere I suspect they utilize for business over leisure. "Nikolaus hasn't let your treatment of his son go uncontested. He's been spreading rumors to other members of the syndicate, the fucking worm."

"Rumors?" Mischa questions, but I can't help feeling that he sounds disinterested. Distracted. I'm not the only one haunted by our last conversation, it seems. "Rumors like his son being a fucking traitor who deserved to be gutted?"

"No." Vanya looks back as if remembering my presence. "Rumors that you…"

"I told you, Vanya," Mischa scolds. "You can speak freely around her."

He sounds so damn smug. Whatever the topic of this conversation is, I suspect that it revolves around me.

"Fine. That prick has been saying that you're too busy fucking Robert Winthorp's leftovers to properly lead. It's gotten the others talking. Some are grumbling that Sergei might be more level-headed—"

"Is that so?" Mischa laughs, stroking his chin. "Maybe it's time to pay Nikolaus a visit? Perhaps later. But for now…"

We round a corner, coming to a narrow room that must be at the very back of the house. Blinds shroud the windows, choking off most natural light. I can only make out the shrouded shapes of various objects. Boxes? Furniture?

"I want to show Little Rose what her life is worth," Mischa declares. He flicks a light switch, flooding the room with the glow from a single lightbulb dangling overhead.

This space might have been a study once, like the one he has upstairs. Now, it's a storeroom containing the mysterious cardboard boxes I spotted in the very first place he kept me after my capture. After approaching one, he pries the lid open and grasps one of the items within.

"Look," he commands, holding it out to me. "Your husband dealt in flesh. But this is what I deal in."

Butterflies squirm to life in my stomach. I don't know what to expect. Cocaine like the awful packets Nicolai possessed? Bloodied coins?

Anything but a long, black object. Its infamous shape leaves no question as to what it is.

"Guns?" I whisper.

According to him, my husband made his fortune on the literal backs of others. How fitting that Mischa trades in violence.

"So unimpressed," he muses as he returns the gun to the box and closes the lid. Is he disappointed? When he captures my chin in his grip, I can't tell. He merely observes me, hunting for secrets within my skin. "The way you act when I say his fucking name…" He chuckles, but there's a harshness to the sound that steals my breath away. "It's like he had you in a fucking cage. But I don't believe that." His nostrils flare as he leans in close. "He kept you so fucking pampered a handful of diamonds wouldn't faze you."

The sound of a throat being cleared makes me jump, and Mischa turns away from me as if realizing Vanya is even there.

"I'm going to track down Nikolaus," Vanya says, his tone gruff. "Before that bastard can spread more lies. In fact, I think you let him off too easy the last time. If his son traded with Winthorp's, who's to say the father didn't, too?"

Mischa's eyes narrow into lethal slits. "Who's to say."

"Then let me handle this." Vanya turns and exits the room.

I make the mistake of thinking we're through and start after him, desperate to retreat to quiet again. Robert, bathe me in gold? Maybe. Gold chains. Golden cuffs. Golden bars over every window.

"Oh no you don't."

I stifle a gasp as Mischa grabs my other arm before I can slip past him.

"I want to know," he snarls against the back of my throat. "I want to know *more*."

About Robert.

"Why?" My voice comes out pained. Afraid? "He's dead—"

"So you keep saying. But he's alive and well in here, Little Rose. Isn't he?" He grips my skull between his hands, applying just a taste of the brute strength he's capable of. "He didn't give you a fucking ring and yet he was willing to kill for you. He hid you. He beat you. Scarred you. Raped you. And yet, every time I'm fucking inside you, I know he's there."

"And if he is?" I spit, exasperated. When he doesn't answer, I can't help scoffing. "What do you want from me?"

His grip tightens, and the room blurs as he drags me into a corner and shoves me against the wall. He gives me no time to regain my bearings. Hot fingers slide around to my front, wrenching at the fastenings of my jeans. Too hard. The clasp breaks, opening me up to a ruthless assault. Then he palms me completely, groaning at the feel.

His hand is too rough. Raw. My breath catches, chest heaving, as individual fingers writhe against my flesh, wringing sounds I don't even recognize from my throat.

"Ride me," Mischa grates into the nape of my neck. "Fuck. Do it."

His index finger parts my folds, flicking in a sinful downward motion. It's like my spine is on a puppet string, controlled by that single, callous touch. Again. Harder. Deeper.

My hips start to rock in time with each motion and he grunts in approval.

But it's still not enough.

Suddenly, his hand withdraws only to tug on my arm, wrenching me around to face him. Shadows exaggerate the amber gaze I've come to fear. A million hidden emotions lurk within it. Demanding things from me. Craving.

But he never says what out loud. He strips me bare instead, shoving his hands beneath my jeans, opening me up to the cock he's palming with trembling fingers. When I start to look down, he grabs my chin, forcing it up. Forcing me to watch him. How his eyes narrow when he sinks into me. The way his nostrils flare with my scent. How he groans at the sinful fit.

His eyelids flutter as he begins to move, thrusting deep. Hard.

Too deep.

"Don't," he warns when my gaze starts to drift. "Look at me. You fucking—" A harsh buck of his hips makes me whine, which almost drowns him out. "Look. At. Me."

Our gazes reconnect and it's like he's in my head more than my body. Boring in too roughly to stop. Showing no mercy. No sanity.

Just taking more. More. More.

My teeth clench around a hollow moan. My knees are jelly, leaving my arms no choice but to grab him for stability. My face aims for his shoulder. I need to hide my gasps. My searing cheeks inflamed with shame for how my body grips him. I need to smother the things I shouldn't feel.

"No." He tilts his head, jarring our noses together. Our mouths. Nipping teeth capture my bottom lip, holding me captive. His eyes are hollow, devouring mine. Something flashes across each fiery iris, gone in an instant. "You've never been this wet for him," he insists between harsh, laving strokes of his tongue. "This loud. Fuck, you're whining for *me*." His eyes close as he savors the high-pitched cries rolling off my tongue.

God, he's moving faster. Harder. I can't breathe.

"You've never needed him like this. Have you?" A brutal thrust makes my vision blur.

Need?

"You were made for this," he tells me. "For *me*." He bucks forward, twitching, straining, spilling.

My thoughts fade. The world spins and spins, and for a split second, my body is the center of the universe. The orgasm slams into me so hard that I can feel the Earth fucking move.

I regain clarity on my hands and knees, gasping on dusty, still air and masculine musk. He's behind me, hunched over my shuddering frame.

"Even now, he's still there," Mischa accuses, nipping at my collar with punishing jabs of his teeth. "Still inside you. Still owning you. I could fuck you for hours and I still couldn't drive him out."

He stands, staggering to find his balance. In seconds, he's redressed, heading for the door.

To leave.

To brood.

Alone.

But something holds him back, making him pause over the threshold.

"Tell me something," he demands, sounding ragged. Empty. Soulless. "If I offered you your freedom. Money. Your fucking soul. Would you ever, for a second, feel for me what you felt for him?"

What I felt for Robert? My blood runs cold, erasing the aftermath of my climax. I shiver at the thought of it, and nothing could disguise the horror that racks my voice. "N-no."

He laughs, even as his eyes darken, sending a chill down my spine. "Why am I not surprised?" He leaves, slamming the door after him.

Angry?

If I felt for him what I felt for Robert…

It would be easier to bear him, certainly.

Because I'd feel nothing.

CHAPTER 9

Mischa is a fickle captor. One moment, he's seemingly merciful, offering my heart's desire. The next, he's content to let me rot.

I'm too tired to put up much of a fight. Instead, I return to my room and curl up on the lone mattress.

My body hums in the aftermath of his violence, like an instrument played to the breaking point—but one used how it's meant to. Ruthlessly thorough. His hands stroke parts of me to exhaustion, making them sing a painful tune.

But it's not music. It's twisted, ugly noise.

In contrast, Robert used me like a tool. His lust was a sledgehammer against a glass nail. Two items well-suited in theory—but in reality, the latter was destined to break. I can't recall the way he felt inside me. I don't want to. Thoughts of him are the remnants of a terrible storm. The details are hazy, but the aftermath is a stark nightmare I'll always relive.

And Mischa wants to be him.

In a funny, terrifying way, it should be easy to swap them out. Pain for pain. Lust for lust. Brutality for brutality.

It should be easy…

But Mischa brings a different kind of agony, so unique that I lack the vocabulary needed to describe it. If Robert had my love, Mischa claims something else. Some hateful part of me I loathe almost as much as I desperately want to feel it. I'm not a numb bird in a cage when he touches me.

I'm a hellcat, aching to scratch him as viciously as he brutalizes me.

In his bed, I'm angry, and vengeful, and *alive*.

Even scarred and brutalized, I can endure every second of his torment.

Maybe the constant game is better than the surrender I'm accustomed to.

At least I'll go insane faster.

What a pathetic creature he's turned me into.

I find snatches of sleep in his absence. When I finally crawl from the mattress, it's dark. Shadows paint the corners of my room and I have to feel my way into the bathroom.

I shower quickly, scrubbing my tormentor away. Naked, I retreat to my bedroom and fish a new outfit from my piles of clothing. My fingers settle rebelliously over one garment in particular: a simple pink dress nearly shapeless in design with a modest neckline.

He accused me of still dressing like I belong to Robert—but when I remember my reasoning for choosing this dress, my husband isn't who comes to mind. Robert liked me swathed in layers and festooned with pretty, frilly things. Lace. Ribbons.

He liked me bundled up like a package only he could tear apart.

This dress? I could smuggle cocaine underneath it in the place of a child if I had to. It would provide sufficient cover if I were locked in an animal's cage, and I could also climb trees in it.

More importantly, a madman could easily slide his fingers beneath it.

And every time I look down at the soft, delicate color, I would remember who I am. *Ellen,* who likes pink. Not because of Briar or Mischa—but in spite of them both.

My fingers shake as I wrench the dress over my head just as sounds drift from the hall. Footsteps. Mischa? Only God knows what new horror he has in store.

I wait, my spine rigid, as the figure advances toward my door and the doorknob rattles. Strange. Vanya knocks, whereas Mischa would just barge in. The second I think as much, the door opens.

A man stands there. He's too thin to be Mischa, his face obscured by shadow.

"I'm supposed to take you to him," he says.

"Who? Mischa?" I take a step forward, so conditioned to follow orders. But then something tugs at the back of my mind and I stop short.

As much as he loathes Robert, Mischa has performed similarly in how he lords his ownership over me. He comes to me himself. Alone. Never before has he sent anyone but Vanya in his place.

I scan the new man more intently, hunting for anything worth noting. Though he's wearing the same gray fatigues as Mischa and his men, I don't recognize his face.

"Where is he?" I ask, not moving another inch.

"He's—" The man cocks his head and suddenly steps farther into the hall. Something about the way he moves makes me creep to the threshold to watch him. He's stiff, marching past another man who rounds the corner. This figure passes me with no interest.

I clench my teeth, uneasy. Is Mischa up to yet another mind game? If he is, I should just retreat to my room. Wait. Hide.

My heart pounds in horror as I enter the hall instead. The unfamiliar man is already halfway to the grand staircase. I presume he'll be descending the steps, but I don't find him in the main entryway. I continue down the hall anyway, toward the dining room. Paces away from the doorway, I hear Mischa.

"Come here."

His irritated tone spurs me closer, but I pause just before entering the room.

"I thought I told you to stay out of here? Don't give me that look," he scolds in a tone so sharp that I flinch. "You're going to hurt yourself if you keep playing with those. Huh? You want to learn to use one?"

I strain my ears, but I don't hear anyone respond.

"I don't think you're ready," Mischa replies to silence.

Is the man truly insane? I inch closer and make out his shape hunched over a glass table in the center of a wide room. In one of his hands is a large knife, which he wields effortlessly.

He tosses it by the handle and catches it, avoiding the blade. "These aren't toys."

Beside him, barely coming to his waist, stands a tiny figure with wild, blond hair spilling over her shoulders. The girl Nicolai wanted used as a drug mule. She watches Mischa intently, and when he catches the knife again, she points to his hand.

"What?" He hefts the blade for her to see more clearly. "You want to try holding it? I don't know… Can I trust you not to cut your damn fingers off?" He laughs and I'm left reeling. Deep and booming, it sounds real.

Insistent, the girl points again.

With a sigh Mischa crouches down to her level and snatches one of her hands. "All right. Hold it like this. Not too tight, but not too loose, either. You drop this and you won't just lose a toe or two, but your whole foot. Understood?"

The girl nods as Mischa adjusts her grip on the blade.

"Now, move your feet. Always brace. Don't think that if you stab something the knife will just go through like paper. You always need force." He makes her sharply jab the tip of the blade into the air and his lips quirk into a satisfied grin. "Like that. Not that you're ready for something like this any time soon."

He stands and takes the knife, returning it to what I realize isn't a table, but a glass case.

"Someone your size needs something smaller," he explains. "I'll see if I can find something later. For now, stay out of this room, got it?" There's no mistaking the authority in his tone, but it's so much softer than I'm used to. He ruffles the girl's hair and she playfully swats him off. "You took the braids out again, I see," he scolds. "As much as you play in the fucking dirt, you keep it clean. If you catch lice, I'll make you sleep with the rest of the stray dogs. Got it?"

The girl's expression conveys something that makes him laugh again.

"Fine. Come here." He sits on an armchair in the corner of the room, and the girl sits on the floor in front of him. Sighing, Mischa smooths back her tangled hair and braids it into a single plait. There's an ease to his movements; he's done this before. "There." He shoos her off with a wave of his hand. "Don't mess it up again. Same goes with the clothes. They belonged to someone special, so don't even think about getting them muddy again."

He bares his teeth, but I marvel at the lack of true anger in his voice. Were he any other man, I'd describe his tone as *playful* even. The girl just grins, scurrying in my direction. Suddenly, her mouth falls flat as she spots my hiding place. She glances back at Mischa but continues down the opposite end of the hall without alerting him.

Alone, I stare, watching him.

He has his face in his hands. In the dim light of the room, his hair gleams, ghosting his shoulders. Like this, it's almost too easy to forget who he is. What he is capable of.

But then he shifts, raising his head and fixating those piercing eyes toward the doorway.

"I gave you permission to scurry around once," he murmurs to the silence. "But I don't remember doing so twice."

Caught, I shuffle forward, entering the room fully. "You called for me," I point out, hating how breathless I sound. Air sticks stubbornly in my lungs, making it a struggle to even form words at all.

"Did I?" He beckons me with a crooked finger and stands. As I near, he grabs my forearm, pulling me even closer. "Now why would I do that?"

His gaze is narrowed. Thoughtful. Alarming. He eyes me the way Robert used to inspect his shooting targets. He'd load his gun, lazily deciding where to aim first.

"To sell me again, maybe?" I gauge his reaction with every word, but he's careful to reveal nothing behind his mocking smile. "To Robert Sr.?"

"And what would the old man want with you?" he asks in a dangerous whisper. "Don't tell me you shared his bed as well?"

He frowns in a way that makes my cheeks flame. He's serious.

"Of course not!"

"Because you were *his*." He nods to himself, as if a suspicion of his has been proven once and for all. "He would have never used you as a decoy, not even for his sister."

"Why does it matter?" I try to wrench my arm back, but his grip tightens and I wind up stumbling into him.

"Because him, I understand, Little Rose," Mischa utters near my ear, his voice cold. "I know your husband. I know how his brain works. But you…" His fingers sink into my hair, grasping strands at random. "You are a mystery that makes no fucking sense."

He lets me go so suddenly that I stagger into the table, forced to brace my hands against it to stay upright. His footsteps advance on me and I sense him standing there, inhaling my scent, breathing out hate.

"You say you love him," he accuses, "but he's hurt you. You jump when I say his name." His touch nudges my spine as if to point out the reaction I wasn't even aware of. "But you call for that fucker in your sleep. You moan for him. Did you know that?"

I didn't. Heat sears behind my eyes as my body stiffens. He's lying. Though maybe he isn't. I haven't remembered a nightmare in years. There's no point. I wake up and purge my soul of anything I might have dreamt of.

Until now.

"I want to know," Mischa demands.

I gasp as his fingers slip beneath my dress, brushing the back of my thigh. Instantly, I regret wearing it. Though, ironically, isn't this one of the many reasons I had in mind for choosing it in the first place?

There's less hassle when his mind switches to sex—which it seems to do so often around me. But as if reading my mind, he grates out a harsh scoff and his nails dig in, making me flinch.

"You play your innocent act. You walk around here, batting your fucking eyelashes, getting Vanya to do your bidding. Was he easier to seduce than I was, Little Rose? Has he tasted you already—"

"Stop!" I push against the table, attempting to flee.

Laughing, he presses harder, grinding my stomach into the wood. "You are very skilled," he insists. "Sometimes, you even have me fooled. Convinced that it's *my* cock getting you off. Making you come. But it's not me, is it?" He grabs the hem of my dress again, lifting it.

"What are you doing?" I try batting his hands away, but he pushes me aside and yanks the dress up further.

"I could understand if he was a normal, pathetic, bleeding-heart motherfucker," Mischa says over me. Our eyes meet and the look in his sends my pulse hammering. "I would understand it. If he never hurt you, I would understand."

Still holding my dress, he brings his free hand to my cheek, nudging my healing wound. "But he did. *This* is me," he says, stroking the outermost edge of the wounds he inflicted. *XV.* Next, he traces the outline of my sore right eye. "So is this. And this…" He moves down to my neck and then my shoulder, aggravating old injuries I'd nearly forgotten. "But *these* are him." His gaze cuts a brazen path down my front, raking over the various scars. "This is him," he snarls, fingering a healed cut along my rib cage. "And this." He turns his attention to my stomach, stroking the length of a raised, silvery scar. "He's hurt you way more than I have."

But Robert had years to inflict his damage. Looking back, only now can I admit that—despite my insistence to the contrary—his true abuse started when I was seven years old and he made me ogle a captive woman for sport.

"And what about you?" I croak, shivering as he meets my gaze directly. "You don't talk about…her. Anna."

The woman who he inferred was his love. I picture her, those wide, brown eyes. With Mischa? It doesn't fit. Not until I envision the boy who crept into a room that he thought was Briar's, intent on using her as a tool in their war. *That* boy would belong with a girl like Anna.

"You say Robert is in my head," I point out when he says nothing. "But you don't mention her. You have no pictures of her—"

"Who says I don't?" His tone sets my nerves on high alert. Dark. Grated. Ragged. "Who says that I don't talk about her? Think about her? Because her memory doesn't rule my life the way your fucking Robert does?"

Danger! I've gone too far. Mischa fists a handful of my dress in both hands, and tearing cotton is my only warning to brace as he tugs. Tears. Strips me bare.

"You think I don't think of her every fucking second of the day?" He doesn't even seem to realize what he's done. What's he's doing: invading my space, crushing me against the table, all while bringing his face within inches of mine. "You think I don't miss her?"

I shove against his shoulders, but he doesn't budge. "N-no."

"No?" He laughs, tossing the remains of my dress to the floor. "She was better than you. Better than you will ever be." He roughly tilts my chin, probing my gaze from a different angle. "She was good, and innocent, and sweet. And your husband destroyed that innocence."

I gasp as he grasps the back of my scalp and wrenches my head back. Eyes streaming, I stare up at the ceiling while his breath fans my exposed throat. Panic renders me motionless —but deep down I know that he could truly hurt me if he wants to.

But he isn't.

"He killed her," Mischa hisses. "And I should have killed you. All this time, I thought it was him. That *he* was a sick, twisted piece of shit who got off on causing pain. But why wouldn't he?"

He tugs harder, turning my face so that my brand is visible. "He had *you.* Fucking him. Moaning in his goddamn ear. Making him feel… Making him feel fucking human."

The way he growls that word in particular resonates in my bones. *Human.*

"You talk about Anna, but you want to know what makes her different from you? She wasn't a cunning little bitch." He pulls harder. Too hard. I claw at his fingers, desperate for relief, but he's impervious to my attempts. "If she were here now, she'd want nothing to do with me. She wouldn't even let me touch her. She'd run. She wouldn't moan for me. She wouldn't compare me to her fucking husband. She wouldn't *look* at me—" He breaks off, inhaling raggedly. He has me pinned against the table's surface, breathing heavily against my throat. "With those fucking eyes. Like you're daring me to just do it already. Wrap my hands around your fucking throat. Squeeze. Put you out of your goddamn misery. You're teasing me, aren't you,

you little bitch?" He sounds crazed. Manic. Laughing, he spits out, "You're taunting me. I'll never fucking have you."

He lets me go, backing away while his fingers fist the air. "Run away, Little Rose," he commands, eyeing me with an unfathomable expression. "*Now.* Get the fuck out!"

I crouch for my dress, only to stare abjectly at the torn pieces of fabric.

"Here!"

I glance up as Mischa shrugs his own shirt over his head and throws it in my direction. Sweat-soaked fabric lands over my knees as he storms past me. "Maybe I'll reconsider selling you after all," he suggests, laughing. "I won't let you play your mind games with me."

The walls tremble with every thunderous step he takes as he retreats down the hall. Numb, I sit here, listening to him travel deeper into the house, trying desperately to anticipate his next move. I can still feel his touch, rough and scraping. Searching.

For what? As I crouch on my knees, shock gradually replaces the hold fear has over my lungs. I start laughing too, cringing at the unstable, high-pitched sound. *Ha ha ha.* Robert could be impulsive when he wanted to be—but even then, I could always predict him. Anticipate him. He liked me meek and pliable, like putty in his hands. Sometimes, he liked it when I put up a fight every now and again.

He never wanted more. He never punished me for not fearing him enough. Fucking him enough. Craving him enough.

Is that what Mischa wants? My blood runs cold as my laughter trails off. I'm shaking, my teeth chattering. Naked, I have no choice but to put his shirt on and hunch beneath the heavy cotton.

He smells so strange: a milieu of nuanced flavors that repulse me and intrigue at the same damn time. When inhaled, they're too complex to describe. This must be what rage smells like. Raw, incredible anger. Twisted musk. Spiteful sweat.

As twisted as he was, I always knew what Robert wanted from me. How to predict him. How to stay alive, even when he became his most unhinged.

But Mischa? There's no fucking point in even trying. He's a storm, changing intensity at his own fucking discretion.

I jump as my own fingers brush my throat, tracing my rapid pulse. He bit me there and the mark stings. Throbs. It's a warning.

Robert brutally scarred my body, but I was still Ellen in the end. Still me.

Mischa is changing me, and I don't know who I'll become when he's through. Someone twisted enough to want…

More.

Enough. I close my eyes, inhaling as much of the stale air as I can until my lungs fully expand. Then I slowly release the breath and reenter the hallway warily, praying that I don't run into Vanya. What would he say if he saw me like this?

Do not fear him. He wasn't always this way…

A flickering shadow draws my notice as I turn into the entryway. Mischa?

The figure lunges before I can be sure. Air whistles past my head, and then… *Pain.* Darkness rushes me, swallowing my vision. A faraway thud echoes as my vision goes white. It's like my senses scatter in a million directions. I feel air. Hardness. Coldness.

Then nothing.

CHAPTER 10

"Wake up!"

Agony rips through my chest, drawing a gasp from my throat. Cool, damp air settles on my face—I must be lying on my back. My head throbs, and my hip is on fire.

"I said wake up," someone snarls. "You little bitch! Look at me!"

My eyelids flutter as I struggle to piece together my surroundings.

Wherever I am, it's dark. Faint light glosses over the hazy outlines of various shapes. One mass in particular looms over me. Tall. Bulky. A man.

But his voice…

It's not Mischa's.

"I said look at me!" Harsh fingers seize my chin, wrenching my gaze toward the figure. His face is familiar. Older. Stern. Dark hair.

A name flickers on the outskirts of my consciousness as a memory of him replays in my head. Him, sitting across from Mischa in a crowded room, while his son, Kostas, was declared a traitor.

"Nikolaus," another man scolds, though I don't recognize his gruffer tone. "If you're going to kill her, do it already. We need to dump her body before Mischa realizes she's gone. Dima said he kept her close. Too fucking close—"

"Kill her?" Nikolaus echoes, his teeth bared. "I'm going to make this little bitch suffer!"

"Use your head," the other man interjects. "I get you want your revenge. But do you really want to fuck with Mischa? That motherfucker will have your head on a spike. Kill her quickly and he won't be able to tie it to you."

"Revenge?" Nikolaus shakes his head. "No!" Grunting, he kicks my hip, knocking me onto my side.

From this angle, I can only watch the muddied tips of his boots move in tandem. Every step echoes, and the air smells damp. Dank. A basement?

I strain my eyes to make out any defining details—and I barely see Nikolaus's foot shoot out to kick me again. Hard. I choke back the scream surging up my throat, but a moan trickles out regardless. Breathing is the only way to regain my composure. *In and out...*

"This little bitch got my son turned into a fucking cripple," Nikolaus rants between heavy pants. "I'm going to rip her apart and drench that whelp Mischa in her fucking blood."

Crippled? Just what did Mischa do to him? Nausea roils through my stomach at the grisly possibilities—I don't want to know.

"Do you know who this bitch is? Who she is really?" Nikolaus laughs, nudging my hip with the tip of his boot. "She was closer to the younger Winthorp than your precious Pakhan let on. Much closer. I know for a fact the bastard wants her back. Rumor is he even offered to trade his sister to Mischa. For this little cunt!"

Another blow draws a groan from my lips, which drowns out whatever he says next. A deafening surge of blood rushes against my eardrums. Bright colors paint my vision. Reds. Greens. Silvers.

Your ribs are broken, a small voice inside me whispers. That's why each breath burns, taking ten times the usual effort.

"I'm not going to kill her," Nikolaus says, his voice drifting back into focus. "I'm going to teach that bastard Mischa why he should never turn on his own fucking kind."

Movement catches the corner of my eye. His boot. As if from miles away, I hear the stomach-churning crack of it connecting with something. Crunching.

Heat runs down my spine like a lance. *Fire.* My vision swims and tunnels; then all senses fade. The terrifying beauty of it is that I feel nothing—even though I'm painfully aware that one of my legs is dragging behind me as I try in vain to crawl away from the source of the assault. The scream that rips from me is more involuntary than anything—my body knows that something is horribly wrong.

"Run, you little bitch," Nikolaus goads as I scrape at the concrete floor in a desperate bid for leverage.

My senses blur and memories meld into the present. I'm with Robert again. He went too far. Again. He's toying with me—*again.*

Running from him will only buy me seconds. I need to plead. Beg. Lie at his mercy and pray to God that he'll stop. Please stop! My lips are already moving to form the words.

"That fucking Mischa thinks he can treat my family like a whipped dog?"

Crunch. Crunch! The veil that shielded my nerves from pain gives way and I feel everything. *Fire, burning agony…*

My thoughts threaten to scatter the second I attempt to focus on it. So I don't. Mischa. His name is like a trigger to all the emotions forbidden to Robert's precious Elle. Hate. Rage. Survival. Above my thudding heartbeat, I can sense that Nikolaus is close, pacing once again.

I try to stand but my limbs refuse to obey the commands my brain issues.

So I crawl, dragging my limp form into a corner. We must be in a basement. The walls are gray gunmetal. Rectangular windows are set high above, revealing pitch-black darkness. In addition to Nikolaus, another man lurks near a shadowed doorway. I vaguely recognize him as well, but I can't place him to a name. Another man from the *mafiya* gathering, maybe?

"Enough," he hisses out when Nikolaus makes his third trip around the room. "Kill her now. You've made your point, and you can laugh yourself to sleep at night when you relive getting one over on Mischa. But do it now—"

"I'm fucking thinking!" Nikolaus tears his fingers through his hair, a wild smile shaping his lips. "Kill her? I could use the little bitch as proof. Mischa's gone insane. This fucking feud. He'll kill us all!"

"He'll kill you," the other man interjects calmly. "If you don't smarten up and take your chance. Who cares if she's important to the Winthorp boy—"

"He might pay for her," Nikolaus muses, stroking his chin. "They say he killed his own father with his bare hands just to get her back. Nearly killed Mischa from what I hear—the bastard refused to give her up."

No. Confusion strikes like a freight train at full force. *Killed his own father…*

The room spins. I can't breathe. An image of a bloodied ring replaces the horrific reality before me, but in some ways, it's so much worse.

"We could sell her to that punk. Make a deal. Teach that bastard Mischa a lesson—"

"He'll kill you," I hear myself croak. God, my voice is a rough, dry whisper. It takes everything I have to make it rise even an octave higher. "He'll make you a deal. Then kill you anyway."

Both men turn their attention to me.

"Shut your fucking mouth!" Nikolaus crosses the room in seconds. His hand lashes out and the world goes black.

I taste blood. When my vision returns, I'm staring at the floor, clutching my jaw. I try to speak but every word comes out garbled.

"Maybe the little bitch is right," the other man says, oblivious to my attempts. "Either way, I say you kill her now. Get it over with."

"I'll do what I fucking want!" Nikolaus shudders, wavering unsteadily on his feet. His eyes reconnect with mine and in them I find nothing. Just hollow emptiness. "I should fuck her," he declares, his tone soft. "Mischa's a jealous little prick. I'll send her back to him. Say she came begging for it—"

"Do you hear yourself, Nikolaus?" the other man asks, but he sounds more impatient than horrified.

Instantly, I know he's no protector. He'll watch. He'll wait.

But I won't be violated again. Not like this.

"You couldn't," I rasp, barely intelligible. But Nikolaus cocks his head, laughing as he tries to decipher my words. "You're…not…man enough."

My brain skips ahead, devising a plan utilizing the only weapon I have left: pride. There was one thing that could make Robert more furious than anything else. One name when mentioned that could make him more skittish and doubtful than a teenage boy during his first encounter.

I suspect that Nikolaus is no different. But where Robert feared his father's presence, this man is terrified of another.

"Mischa is twice the man you are." The pathetic, broken creature speaking doesn't even sound like me—she's bolder than I ever was.

"What did you say?" Nikolaus advances, his fingers curling.

"I said you couldn't even come close to him—"

"Shut up!"

Lightning. I see it. Taste it—coppery, wet warmth dripping off my tongue.

"Look at me, you little cunt! You think you've handled a real fucking man?"

My heart stutters as fabric tears nearby. Cold air assaults my body a second later.

I've failed. Failed. He's already crouching over me, spreading my legs apart.

Breathe, a part of me whispers, clinging to my old mantra. *You can survive this, Ellen. Just breathe...*

Or I can fight.

My eyes stream as I crane my neck, repulsed by what I see. His pants are down, his palm clenching his cock. I override every instinct urging me to scream and I…

Laugh. Loudly. Hard. I cackle mercilessly even as I lose feeling in my toes. Fingers. Arms. An invisible vise is tightening around my chest with every second. Blood floods my mouth.

You're dying, that honest voice in my soul hisses.

When Nikolaus curses, I know I've succeeded in one aspect so far. Men like him can't bear being taunted. They feed off fear and cowering.

So I force my tongue to move and mock him instead. "I… was…wrong. You aren't even a fraction of the man Mischa is."

How ironic that thinking of him anchors me when my thoughts fight to fade and my limbs grow heavier. Mischa, my tormentor. He'll chase me into the grave.

God, it's like I fucking hear him. Shouting. Roaring…

Pounding?

A man groans amid a crunching thud of bone. Suddenly, Nikolaus is gone and someone new takes his place, crouched over me.

"Look at me, Little Rose," he demands, haloed by a wreath of wild, golden hair.

My eyelids flutter. I'm dreaming.

"Look at me. You fucking hear me? You can sink into the black. Think you can run from me… But you'll die when I say you can, Ellen Winthorp. And I'm not done playing with your fucking soul just yet."

CHAPTER 11

Numb limbs weigh me down in a sea of endless black. I feel nothing. Hear nothing…

At least at first.

Eventually, snippets of sound and scattered phrases puncture the silence.

Broken ribs.

Shattered femur.

Broken ankle.

Dying.

Dying.

"Open your eyes, Little Rose," the devil growls.

How fitting that my soul would be claimed by him.

"Open your fucking eyes. I know you're still in there. I'm waiting. So open your fucking eyes…"

But even he can't keep me grounded for long. My soul is tissue paper, caught between two unreachable worlds. One is bright and soft. It calls to me in delicate whispers.

Come home.

The other is dark, and painful, and loud. So damn loud. It snarls into my ear, increasingly incessant.

"Look at me, Little Rose. Open your fucking eyes…"

I long to sink into the warm light and forget the madness, and the torment, and the pain. So much fucking pain.

Death is so quiet…

But a world containing Mischa is impossible to ignore. He drags me back, bit by bit until sensation returns in agonizing snatches. I can't move. I'm lying on my back, aware that I'm on a mattress. Light and shadow flicker behind my eyelids as people move nearby. Talking.

"I thought I told you not to come in here?" a man scolds, but his tone is gentle. And familiar, though I've never heard it so hoarse. "You wanted to braid her hair again?"

He pauses, but no one responds.

"Fine," the man says, sighing. "But you're going to make her bald."

Me? My head throbs, but through the pain, I sense a gentle touch moving through my hair, gathering up various strands and carefully arranging them.

"Don't give me that look," the man says, and I can finally put a name to that husky rasp. Mischa? "For a girl, you have an odd idea of what looks pretty. And you're lucky I'm even letting you stay after what you did with the crayons—" He breaks off as if interrupted. Then he laughs. "Keep it up and I'm going to sell you right back to Nicolai."

Sell? I try lifting my eyelids. Moving. Speaking. Even breathing is a struggle. Mischa must have devised a new form of torture: sitting on my chest.

"Don't stay in here too long," he warns amid the thud of heavy footsteps. "And no more fucking coloring."

He's gone, but I'm not alone. Someone continues to stroke my hair, styling it with all the care that I used to take with Briar's. Vanya?

Again, I try opening my eyes. At first, I can only make out snippets of detail. White walls bathed in daylight. Crisp ivory sheets. A bulky, round shape that I think is my leg propped on a pillow.

Straining with the effort, I manage to hold my eyes open long enough to acknowledge that I'm in a small room, on a bed positioned near a row of wide windows overlooking a swath of green. There's a doorway up ahead, leading into shadow. Someone's perched beside me on the mattress, partially visible: tiny legs sheathed in oversized pants and slender arms that go still the moment the figure must realize I'm awake.

I'm jostled as the slender person in question leaps from the bed. In a blur, they race from the room. Pale. Blonde. The little girl from Nicolai's.

I try to sit up only to wheeze, my eyes watering as the pressure in my chest tightens. Mischa isn't sitting on me after all. Vaguely, I remember being struck. Beaten. By Nikolaus.

He broke my ribs, I think.

And my leg. Both of them, it seems. One is encased in a bulky cast, propped upright, while a neat array of bandages covers the other. My blankets have been pulled back to reveal both, including the strange purple markings marring my cast. I scan them all, increasingly confused. One drawing consists of a lopsided smiley face. Another is of a crudely etched tree. And finally, a man with long, squiggly hair and exaggerated magenta eyes glares at me from the space near my ankle.

I stiffen as someone approaches, traipsing down what I assume is a hallway. Two footsteps, one light and swift, the other heavy and slow.

"What is it?" Mischa grumbles. "If you drew on the goddamn cast again, I swear I'll—" He breaks off the second he rounds the corner, spotting me awake.

By his side, leading him by the sleeve of his shirt is the girl from Nicolai's.

"I see." Mischa's expression falls into the stern mask I know so well. "Leave." He wrenches his arm from the girl.

Despite the authority lacing his tone, she lingers, watching me with wide, owl-like eyes.

"Go," he snarls more harshly, and she finally scurries off.

Alone, my captor watches me with an unreadable gaze, and paranoia eats at my pain. How often has he lorded over me like this? Waiting for me to die. Daring me to.

Silently, he advances. Outstretched fingers reach for my cheek, but I turn away, gritting my teeth. My jaw is so sore that a moan escapes when I don't mean to do it.

Mischa draws his hand back anyway, his eyes narrowing. Then he turns and leaves without a word.

CHAPTER 12

I must fall asleep. When I come to again, someone is spooning warm liquid against my lips, encouraging me to swallow.

"Nice and easy," they urge. Vanya.

I fight through a layer of exhaustion to open my eyes, meeting his startled expression.

"That's it," he praises as I sip from the spoon. "Now, just rest."

It's so easy to surrender to his care, letting myself drift off once again.

When I open my eyes a second time, something is different. The pain has lessened, for one, and I can haul myself upright, bracing my trembling hands on either side of my body for balance. I'm alone as well. What I first mistook for a hospital room must be just another part of Mischa's manor. I recognize the dreary lawn from the windows, and the furniture has the same stifling, ornate air to it.

However, I'm on an unfamiliar bed from my usual mattress. Someone changed the sheets while I was out, exchanging the white ones for a softer gray. They changed me as well.

Once… Years ago, Robert hit me harder than he meant to. I wound up in bed for weeks, forced to endure a painful recovery. Out of duty, or maybe guilt, Robert had an army of servants provide me with round-the-clock care.

But none of them bathed my skin with scented soap. Or washed my hair so that it smelled faintly of fresh flowers. Or kept me so clean that I didn't feel like an invalid.

But I was. I am. A metal tray stands a few paces from the bed, complete with a steaming meal someone must have been in the process of feeding me. Memories return as cloudy, intangible snippets: soups and broths carefully poured down my throat while I was barely conscious.

By Vanya? Only he would have the patience. The care.

Only he would be so kind.

Gratitude unlike anything I've ever felt swells in my chest, making it even harder to breathe. Nikolaus inflicted his damage well. I wonder if the bastard is in hell.

Because he most certainly isn't still alive. I'm sure of it, just as I'm sure that Mischa is watching me. I can't see him yet, but I smell him. Lurking near the doorway maybe?

After swiping my tongue along my dry lips, I croak, "I know you're there."

God, I sound horrible. So pathetically weak. Pity must be what makes him drop his ruse and finally round the edge of the doorway.

My eyes widen at his appearance. It has to have been days since I last saw him. The stubble growing in along his jaw is thicker. Scraggly. Unkempt. His hair is a messy, unwashed tangle, his clothing a pair of faded fatigues.

"So," he begins in a low, gruff tone, "Little Rose has finally decided to grace us with her miraculous return."

Finally. The emphasis he placed on that word draws my attention. "How…" I wheeze as my chest constricts and take my time forming my next words. "How long was I out?"

"A month," he says, shrugging. "Maybe more than that. Your injuries were stabilized within a few days, but you…" He grunts a sound that could be mistaken for a laugh had it come from any other man. "The stubborn, spiteful Little Rose wouldn't let a mere doctor dictate her recovery."

He enters the room and his scent descends at full force. Sweat and animalistic musk. How long has he been there, watching me? Long enough, a part of me suspects. Long enough to immediately go to the food and wrestle the tray closer.

My stomach grumbles, embarrassingly loud, but when he shoves a spoonful of broth beneath my nose, I shake my head, choosing to speak instead.

"You…lied."

He drops the spoon into the bowl, spraying broth across the tray's surface. "Did I now?"

But it's a reality that haunted me, even as my soul drifted for days at a time.

"Robert," I rasp. "He's alive. You lied to me. He's *alive*."

Fire ignites in my jaw and I gingerly reach up, brushing my fingers along the sore tissue. Even that slight motion takes more energy than I have in me. Groaning, I slump back against a wall of pillows, forced to view Mischa from a newer angle.

He's chuckling, his gaze averted away from me. Down at his hands. The nails are ragged, with a dark substance caught beneath them. Dirt? Or Blood?

"Does his life matter to you that much?"

I frown, caught off guard by the venom in his tone. "*You* told me he was dead."

"And as concerned as you are for your husband's welfare, you should be more concerned for yours."

Concerned? I open my mouth to reply, but he moves, wrenching the blankets back.

"Look," he commands.

Startled, I stare down at my pale limbs stretched out beneath a white nightgown. My legs aren't the only parts of me bandaged: my nightgown has been folded down to my waist, but my chest isn't bare. Tan bandages constrict it—part of the unbearable pressure I feel.

"You were intubated for three days," Mischa announces. "Your lung was punctured. It's barely healed. So I suggest you save the sobbing for your husband's soul for another week at least—"

"What happened to Nikolaus?"

"What he deserved," he says. "And you have another surgical scar to join the one from your C-section, Little Rose."

I cringe at the reference, but the painful memories are easier to ignore in favor of deciphering him. His voice is colder than it was only a few minutes ago. Irritated.

Scowling, he tugs my blankets back into place, covering me again. "If you won't eat, I can assure you that you'll be here for another fucking month. Though, hell, that might make it easier for your precious Robert to come for you?"

I'm too tired to feel the full brunt of the terror that threat should inspire. I just let my eyes drift shut and focus on breathing. In. Out. Slower. When I feel confident enough to speak, I don't even waste any real effort on sounding insulted. "Where is Vanya?"

It's like my words are his cue. Another figure approaches from the hall, his steps uneven.

"You're awake," he calls as I open my eyes again. His wary smile is a godsend. Even Mischa's brooding presence can't erase my relief.

"Thank you," I tell him as he draws up to the other side of my bed. "For caring for me."

Even now, the gentleness with which he must have done so takes my breath away. A month in bed could have gone so much worse. That I know from experience.

Vanya blinks. "I…" His gaze cuts to Mischa, who abruptly storms from the room. "I'm glad you're all right," Vanya says, turning his attention back to me. "You had us worried."

Us? I don't question the word choice out loud. Instead, I watch him circle around to the tray of soup. He carefully ladles a bit of broth to my lips and I swallow. When I've consumed half the bowl, I gather up the nerve to finally ask, "Did Mischa kill him?"

Nikolaus.

"Yes," Vanya says as he maneuvers another spoonful to my mouth. His gaze turns inward, alarmingly stern. "The bastard had it coming. I still don't know how he infiltrated the manor. He wasn't that smart—"

"Someone else was there," I rasp. "Another man. He talked about…" I rack my brain for the specifics. "He talked like he knew some details firsthand."

"So a spy," Vanya deduces, his gaze cold. "I'll alert Mischa. But you shouldn't have to worry about this." A sigh rips from his mouth as he sets the bowl aside. "You get your rest. I'll come check on you in the morning."

He gathers up the empty bowl and leaves, avoiding any further questions. Alone, I can only anticipate Mischa's next actions.

I've angered him, and a sick part of me wonders if I should be relieved.

At least I'll no longer be his focus.

CHAPTER 13

"Get up."

I know instantly that Vanya isn't the figure I awaken to find standing above me.

Mischa's clean shaven, his face pale in the dim glow of dawn. Somehow, he looks more unstable this way. Dark circles paint the flesh beneath his eyes, and a muscle in his jaw twitches once he catches me staring.

"The man you say you saw. Did you get a name?"

"What?" My eyebrows furrow. "I…"

"I guess not." He scoffs, radiating suspicion. "Maybe you'll remember when that cunning brain of yours decides it's in your best interest? No matter. It's time for *Vanya* to give you your bath. You stink."

I do. Like sweat, from tossing uncomfortably all night. I smell like fear of what might lurk beneath my scars. I smell like Robert's wife again.

"Where is he?" I anxiously scan the room for Vanya, but Mischa yanks the blankets from me instead.

He nudges the pillow from under my casted leg and slides a hand beneath both.

I suck in a startled breath. "What are you doing?"

Without warning, he pulls me into his arms.

"S-stop!" I cling to his shoulders—but he isn't being rough. Not even as he swiftly carries me into a hallway.

We don't go far. A few doors down from the bedroom, he turns into one bathed in shades of black. His.

He takes me into the bathroom, where running water is filling a sunken tub. A plastic bench is positioned beside it, and an array of tools are within reach. But the man who sets me down and tears at my thin nightgown isn't the patient, calm Vanya.

Tension stiffens his posture as he snatches up a rag and wets it.

"Lift your arms," he grates.

I want to refuse, but curiosity is a strange thing.

He starts to wash me without waiting for me to comply, dragging the rag over my exposed thigh. His teeth are gritted, his eyes downcast. But even so…he's careful. Clinical.

And now I know just who cared for me all these weeks.

The thought of it weighs me down with an unexplainable emotion. Shock? Perhaps. Or maybe resignation to one simple fact I'm too tired to resist: I'll never fully understand him.

And I'm not sure if it's a good thing.

Or horrifying.

"Lift your arms," he commands through gritted teeth.

I obey, alarmed to find that I can only raise the limbs to the height of my shoulder without triggering pain. As Mischa peels down my nightgown and starts to unravel the bandages, I see why. Beneath carefully placed gauze is a half-moon-shaped ridge of reddened flesh.

Punctured lung, he said. The kind of injury that I doubt could be safely treated in a mobster's safe house.

"Was I in a hospital?"

Mischa continues to tug my nightgown off, lifting me with one hand to pull the fabric free.

"I have power everywhere, Little Rose," he says. Power, meaning control. Spies. A presence, should I ever think of running away again.

Warm water spilling across my lap alerts me to the fact that he's still washing me, guiding the cloth against the bruised flesh of my hip. I suck in a breath and he pauses, letting liquid drip from the rag onto the floor.

"I killed him," he says, so low that I barely hear him. "With my bare fucking hands."

I close my eyes against the imagery, but it's no use. I see Mischa, his hands drenched in blood, his teeth bared, his eyes flashing with crazed menace. And his voice… Something in the cold, satisfied tone he used makes my lips spring apart, rebelling against my common sense warning me to stay silent.

"Is that supposed to impress me?"

"It doesn't," he says, sounding unsurprised.

The rag returns to my hip and I jump, anticipating roughness. His pressure, however, never changes, even as his eyes darken.

"One man's death would never impress the innocent Little Rose—"

"No one's death would impress me."

"Oh?" He laughs. "You're wrong. For all your games, I won't let you deny it now: All along, deep in your fragile, little soul, you knew he wasn't dead. You tried resisting it." He nods to my severed finger. "But you knew. And though you won't say it out loud, you're glad he's still alive. Why?" he asks when I say nothing. "Because for all your fucking insistence to the contrary, you want to see him choke out his last fucking breath for yourself. You won't believe it until you do. And you don't want it any other way. Your precious Robert dies when you say he can. Isn't that right, Little Rose?"

Rather than humor him with an answer, I close my eyes and cling to my one and only escape. *Breathe.* My nostrils flood with the steam from the running bath and the musk of his sweat, tainted with something sweeter. He scented the water with something. Oil? Soap? It smells like lavender, whatever it is. I can't ignore it.

That stench makes all of this feel so fucking real. A nightmare wouldn't be perfumed with flowers. Mischa's touch wouldn't be gentle over my bruised, broken limbs.

My heart wouldn't be swollen with conflicting emotions, and tears wouldn't be forming behind my eyes, desperate to fall.

I try to breathe, but in the end, all I can do is voice a plea that comes out as a whisper. "I don't need your help."

"Fine."

My eyelids jolt upright as water splashes nearby. He threw the rag into the tub. Without looking back, he stands and marches to the door. Then he wrenches it open and slams it shut behind him. Beneath the pulse of rushing water, I hear myself wheeze as I try to catch my breath. Air is a fickle, elusive thing, rebelliously escaping my lungs.

Maybe I'm afraid. I want to be. Terror is much more preferable to guilt. Shame. Regret.

I attempt to bend for the rag, but it's too far. I can't reach the faucet, either—not that I'm left floundering for long. Mischa is like a dog. He'll run away when spooked, only to circle back snarling, twice as aggressive as before.

"Sit up," he commands, storming back into the room. He switches off the running water and snatches a new rag from a stack placed just beyond reach of the bench.

As I struggle to haul myself upright, he sinks to his knees and returns to washing me. He's never too rough or intentionally causes pain. But his shoulders are rigid, his eyes downcast and stormy.

Consoling him feels more like a necessary survival tactic than any form of pity.

"Thank you," I rasp as he stands and circles the bench. Warm water grazes my back next, soothing aches I didn't even know I had. "For washing me—"

"For filling in for *Vanya*, you mean?" His nasty tone betrays an emotion I don't even think he's aware of. Could it be wounded pride? "Let's agree on something, Little Rose."

He throws the rag down beside me and crouches low again, this time right near my side so that every word strikes my throat in a burst of heat.

"I know you want to be the helpless victim, and I am more than willing to indulge you." He drags his thumb across my cheek, but there is no clinical care this time. He makes me flinch and smiles when I do. Despite the quirk of his lips, nothing reaches his eyes. They're endless, fiery pits. "You willingly played the part of your husband's dutiful doll… and now, you're mine. I'll make you dance and scream how I want to. I'll keep you close, Ellen. So fucking close…" He's nearer, murmuring each word in my ear. "I'll make you choke on me. You'll fucking hate me—but not because of him. Because you'll need me more. You can't fucking breathe without me."

He rises to his feet and approaches the tub. After testing the water with his fingers, he cuts his gaze in my direction. Then he takes his shirt off before tossing it into a corner of the room.

My heart races with every step he advances toward me in no apparent rush. When he grabs me, I tense in anticipation of a pain that never comes.

He's done this before. I'm sure of that one fact as he places me on the floor beside the tub and begins to encase my cast in something. Plastic. He secures it tightly over the entire plaster. Then he starts to unravel the bandages on my other leg. It must not be as injured as the other, just badly bruised. Sprained, I suspect when I wiggle the toes and wince as lightning-sharp heat surges through the muscle.

I'm resigned to the crippling senses of immobility when he lunges, plunging into the bath despite still wearing his slacks. The next second, I'm in his arms again.

My stomach lurches up my throat as my lower half descends into the warm liquid. I flail, my arms splashing uselessly as my head goes under. Water floods my nostrils, overwhelming my weak lungs—for a second. The next, I'm held tight against a firm, searing surface. Mischa. I'm clinging to him, my nails scraping against his forearms for leverage. Gasping, I find that he's holding me at an angle, placing more of my upper body into the water while leaving my leg exposed and supported by the edge of the tub.

And now I understand what he means.

His doll.

At his mercy.

At his whims.

He keeps me in the tub just long enough to douse me thoroughly in the places his rag won't reach. My hair. Between my legs. My once-bandaged leg. Water stings as it sweeps against my injuries, but when my eyes start to water, he carries me from the tub and returns me to the bench.

He towels me off in silence, and I'm forced to bear his resentment. It's only when he leaves the room and returns with a garment dangling between his fingers that I lose my resolve. I sigh.

"Lift your arms," he tells me, bringing the nightgown close.

A creation formed of light-pink silk, it looks like something Briar would wear—as a joke. Something too frilly even for Robert's taste. A mocking caricature of what a living doll might be adorned with: white lace and pink ribbons.

Once I'm dressed, Mischa returns me to the large, white room. The sheets on the bed have been changed, the air scented. Every seemingly kind gesture only unnerves me more. Especially one small detail that catches my eye as I'm lowered to the mattress: He leaves space beside me. The bed is large enough for him to do so, with room to spare, but an extra set of pillows have been placed beside mine. The tray that I assume is for my meals has been moved from its position near the wall toward the opposite end of the room, closer to me.

Leaving the remaining half as the dominion of one person.

He doesn't say it out loud, not yet. He yanks the covers over me and exits the room without hinting at his true motives.

But Mischa Stepanov is quickly becoming as familiar to me as a damaged, twisted book I have no choice but to study. He'll be back.

Sooner or later, he'll be back.

He lets me luxuriate in the uncomfortable reality of being his doll. For the most part, it's rather boring, no different from my life with Robert. In short, I'm left alone to rot in a room I can't explore, utterly at his mercy.

Are physical limitations so different from mental ones?

I'm not brave enough to decide on an answer, and approaching footsteps draw my attention, giving me a small reprieve.

Vanya enters the room, carrying a tray between his hands. Another bowl of soup and a thin slice of bread. After perching himself on the end of my side of the bed, he feeds me slowly. All without a word.

Even though there's something he wants to say.

I can practically see the words straining in his throat, fighting to lurch off the end of his tongue. In the end, he pats the blankets covering me and leaves.

As he fades into the shadow beyond the doorway, I know exactly what he left unsaid. He wanted to warn me.

Of all of his whispered insights into Mischa, one rings the loudest in my memory. *"If he thinks you're worth having, he will never let you go."*

If only it were me he really wants. I'm an expert at selling myself. Molding myself. Suppressing myself. I've done it for years under the watchful possession of Robert. Hell, if my life was reversed, I might do it all over again. It's easy to sacrifice that which you've never really had in the first place.

From the day I was born, I was always a burden, forced to hide. Pretend. Submit.

But Mischa… He wants something else. Something more than anyone has ever demanded of me before. Something raw and unguarded, found in the sleep he wrings from me. Something I can't change, or morph, or control.

I think he wants my soul.

Not to keep, but to break—right between the rough, callused fingertips that graze my forehead, rousing me from a fitful sleep.

It's darker in the room now. Not quite night, but close. My stomach rumbles, though not from hunger. Just an uneasy apprehension of the unknown.

He switches a light on. With his back to me, he starts to pace. Then he lifts his shirt over his head and tosses it onto the floor. I hear the zipper of his jeans come undone next.

And I'm breathless, gulping at the thinning air. It never ceases to amaze me just how beautiful he is—or what some might call him anyway. How rugged. He is scarred over and broken in so many places, I wonder if he remembers what the original flesh and bone look like. The marks of his brand gleam silver in the orange glow of a lamp. VII. They ripple with his every movement, proclaiming his place in the feud as he removes his pants one leg at a time and stands there only in a pair of gray boxers.

He waits as if to torment me, stretching out the seconds, ensuring I'm riveted for every torturous one. Eventually, he cocks his head, finding my position. It's unfair how quickly he moves, denying me the chance to gather my senses or play my part by cowering. He's lying beside me before I even remember to cringe beyond his reach. One of his hands grasps mine, forcing it to his chest.

At first, I think it's a perverted mind game designed to test my reaction. But no. He wants me to feel. Ropey, jagged skin dips and curves beneath my fingertips. His wound from the day he delivered "Robert's" ring.

"Your husband fought for you, Little Rose," he tells me, his voice thicker than I've heard it. "He fought like hell for you. Enough to dirty his pretty little hands." He grips mine roughly, unfolding every digit for his inspection. "Shall I tell you all of it? He offered to trade you for Briar—to give me better leverage with his father, you see. I didn't think he was serious, but she was there..." He laughs brokenly, shaking his head. "But I refused. And he tried to kill me. We've met before, you know. I've baited him before. Taunted him before..." He trails off, lost in a thought I can't stomach to consider.

Regardless, his words fester and stew within me. Robert fight for me? Never.

"He did," Mischa challenges as if reading my mind. "That fucker was willing to die for his precious little wife. But I won, didn't I, Little Rose? Even if I left his fucking life intact. I have you..."

My heart clenches before I even feel a telltale brush of warmth against my throat: his mouth, murmuring words there in a dangerous whisper. "I have you, don't I? All of you. Even if you don't want it." He shifts, sliding one of his hands beneath my blankets, aiming for my inner thighs.

Weighed down by my cast, I can't even move. I just stiffen as he finds me beneath my nightgown, inching higher with every strained breath I take.

"Even if you can't admit it. I have you. I can keep you. Or I can kill you."

Air wheezes from my lungs as he slides the ridge of his finger against me. Inside me. My heart churns uselessly as my chest tightens. The sensation of his touch works like an invisible vise, tightening. Smothering. Suffocating.

I pant. "M-Mischa—"

"He killed his father for you. Do you know that?"

My thoughts swim. My head feels heavy. Air becomes a scarcer commodity. Frantic, my fingers scrape at the blankets beside me. "Please—"

"The bastard never dared to stand against the old man before." His voice is my only anchor as his touch grows bolder and my vision narrows. A gray haze shrouds everything but his face, half obscured against my breast, laughing at the dark irony. "I told him I strangled you," he admits, sounding miles away.

Everything is white. Then gray. Then quiet…

Finally, air! I gulp noisily for every breath as his hand withdraws.

"He hasn't come for me yet," Mischa grumbles, more to himself than me. "But he will."

He watches me collapse against the pillows as I strain my lungs as much as my sore chest allows. Finally, he moves, but not to retreat. Oh, no. He tilts my head toward him as he settles further on the mattress beside me.

"Shall I tell you a story, Little Rose?" he murmurs, only to force my head to nod in agreement. "Fine, then. You ask me how I can care for you so well? I was number seven, but there was an eight... Her name was Aljona and she was better than you in every way. Sweeter. Kinder. She deserved mercy where your precious Winthorps deserve none." He waits, allowing every word to sink in. Every insinuation. He lets my mind race to put the pieces together: the real woman who haunts him. Not Anna. Not even his mother.

"She was my half," he rasps brokenly as heat springs beneath my eyes. "We shared a womb. A soul. Your Winthorps left her for dead when they forced the car my mother was driving into a ditch. They left her twisted and broken in the wreckage when they took my mother and me, but she survived, Little Rose. She clung to life…until it became too fucking much."

He's on his feet, halfway across the room before I can even register the vicious steps that take him there.

"When she died, *I* died, Little Rose." His back is to me, his posture rigid. "So don't for a second make the mistake of believing that anything I've done is for you. You're merely meant to serve a fucking point: Even now, I'm not like them. I won't let you compare me to him." He laughs and braces a hand against the wall. For balance, I realize. He's shaking, trembling from head to toe.

It's terrifying. Like witnessing the worst dredges of a storm unfold with no hope of shelter within reach. Emotion from him is a drug: a terrifying injection of toxins and hallucinogens. I see things I shouldn't. Experience sensations that aren't real.

Mischa…moaning in pain isn't real.

I blink and he's upright, his bloodshot eyes finding me from over his shoulder.

"You want to stay a shell? I'll make you a fucking proxy. You can die here for all I care."

And he means it. Every word rings true as he dresses himself and leaves.

He didn't save my life out of any ounce of human pity.

He did it as a test.

And he failed.

CHAPTER 15

Vanya greets me in the morning, and he's the one who helps me bathe with as much dignity as I can muster. There's a notable difference though.

Vanya is clinical.

Mischa was…methodical. Damn near obsessive, even—like my body was a tool he'd studied every inch of. A collector, polishing his favorite toy.

I'm sweating beneath the sheets. The air in this room has little circulation, and a part of me longs for the warmth of bathwater. A change of scenery.

Anything.

Vanya does his best to linger, entertaining me with small talk, but he can't stay long.

And I'm alone again.

It's the loneliness that feels so different from my time with Robert. I used to crave it. Cherish it. Only in silence could I gather up the broken pieces of my soul and try to reassemble them. I was Ellen, always Ellen. Sweet, dutiful, doormat Ellen.

It's only hours after Vanya delivered my second meal for the day that I sense someone else there, lingering on the outskirts of my room, recognizable only by smell.

He waits like any predator, anticipating the moment I tense with an awareness of him. Maybe he can hear my pulse surging in a pathetic patter of noise. When the symphony of heartbeats reaches a crescendo, he steps forward.

From my position, I can only make out his profile. Long and unkempt, his hair shrouds most of his face, leaving the rest of it cast in shadow. The stubble has returned already to coat his chin, which flexes as he prepares to issue a command or another insult.

Hoarse and weak, my pathetic tone beats him to the punch. "I can't live like this."

He jerks in place as if he'd been about to lunge. Pounce. Attack. Now? He stands there, his head cocked.

"I can't," I admit, hating the fear so plainly evident in my voice. Leaving any part of myself bare to him disturbs me like nothing else. But it's better than the alternative: this fucking endless silence. "I refuse to live like this—"

He turns for the door and I can't stop myself from leaning forward, clutching fistfuls of the sheets for balance.

"Please…"

He stops and I break.

"*Please* don't let me live like this. I'm sorry if I hurt you—if I *insulted* you," I add when he flinches. "But I'm so damn tired of begging you for mercy."

He stays just long enough to give me hope that my words managed to reach him before he slips over the threshold and escapes the room.

For the rest of the day, I'm left here, alone, trapped in bed, forced to listen to the ongoings of the manor seeping through the walls. Murmured snippets of conversation provide no context. No reprieve.

Eventually, I tune the noise out altogether and turn my focus toward gingerly stretching and flexing each limb, desperate to move. A funny thought makes me snicker as the daylight grows dimmer and Vanya appears with my evening meal.

Of all the various forms of torture Robert employed to break me, this might do the trick.

Sheer, utter boredom.

I'm startled awake by the sound of footsteps nearing my bed. Heavy and slow, they aren't Vanya's. Neither is the hand that snatches my blankets from me, leaving me shivering in the pale glow of dawn. The rest of the house can't be up this early.

Though I suspect that the figure before me hasn't slept at all.

He's silent as he slides a hand beneath my legs and lifts me from the bed. I settle awkwardly in his arms, aware of just how stiff he is against me. Still angry. Still fuming.

Still gentle.

A part of me marvels at that. Robert didn't have an ounce of the same control. Which made him easier to handle in a way. I could talk him down with a few groveling words at a time and all would be well—until the next time.

But Mischa broods. In some ways, he reminds me of a child, preferring to stew in his temper—because the alternative requires swallowing his pride and assessing his own actions.

So, instead, he ignores them stubbornly and I'm the one to suffer.

I stiffen as he carries me down the hall and into yet another bathroom. The bench has been moved here, with all the supplies neatly placed within reach, but the tub is bigger. Deeper. Already half-filled with water, it triggers my alarm like nothing else.

He could drown me.

Ironically, Mischa seems oblivious to the dark scenarios my mind conjures. He sets me down and wets a rag. Silently, he tugs my nightgown off and laves my skin with quick, efficient strokes. Watching him, I notice every nuance in him that I otherwise wouldn't. How tightly he grips the rag, for one—so hard that his knuckles whiten. How his shoulders ripple, distorted by bulging, tensing muscle.

He doesn't notice the moment I touch him, laying my fingers along his wrist. Not at first. He's that intent on ignoring me. Beneath my fingertips, I feel him suddenly jerk and he wrenches the arm away. Flashing, his eyes cut up to mine as his lips spring apart.

But I speak first. "How long until I can walk?"

He frowns, but just as quickly, his mouth quirks into a disarming smirk. "Who says I'll let you?"

He's joking. He has to be… The second I start to suspect the opposite, he lets the expression fall and returns his focus to the rag.

"The doctor will be here to see you again in a week, Little Rose. Work your charms on him and I'm sure he'll try to steal you away. You'll have your freedom in no time—"

"I don't like it when you mock me." I'm surprised by how strongly my voice comes out.

"Mocking?" He scoffs and observes me, his head tilted. "Oh no, Little Rose. I'm *predicting*. It seems that you have a knack for winning powerful men to your side."

There it is again. That prickling note of jealousy that seems so out of place in his gruff baritone.

"I don't want to play this game with you—"

"Game?" Mischa laughs. "Oh no, this isn't a game to you. This is life. Vanya pities you, but I *know* you. I know how you could survive a man like Robert Winthorp all these fucking years. You crawled inside his head like a parasite—"

"Robert is who he is without me," I counter. "I didn't make him do a damn thing."

"Oh really? Then you don't know the bastard as well as you claim to. And I'm starting to think he never knew you, either. His precious wife, a snake—"

"And you're a murderer."

"A murderer…" His eyes widen, and then he nods, chuckling. "Yes. Most recently for you. Isn't that right?" He fingers a strand of my hair, twisting it around his finger. Leaning close, he murmurs near my ear, "I killed Nikolaus for *you*."

"And again, I ask: Is that supposed to impress me?"

"It doesn't," he admits, his mouth tilted in amusement. "But you are used to grander displays of affection, aren't you? Men who parade you before their fucking captives for sport."

"Stop!" My heart races as my throat resonates with the force of the shout. Mischa has the rag against my thigh and I shove his fingers away. "Don't touch me."

"You really want to go through this again?" He drops the rag into the water and stands. "Be my fucking guest."

But he doesn't leave. He's there near the door, watching. To mock me. To gloat.

"You want to know the real difference between you and Robert?" I croak, knowing he can hear me. Goading him is a dangerous, foolish act—but I can't stop myself. My eyes burn as I shift my weight as much as I dare. My bandaged foot might be able to bear weight. Gingerly, I lower it to the floor, guiding my thigh between my hands. I tentatively bear down and the knee buckles. "He is selfish," I say, gritting my teeth in frustration. My body is too weak to stand.

So I'll crawl.

I don't think about the pain or the potential consequences of injuring myself further. Clenching my jaw, I throw my weight to one side of the bench and brace myself with my hands. Sure enough, the bench topples beneath me and a monstrous crash echoes throughout the room. Pain scars along my side, but I can still move.

"He is selfish," I repeat, dragging myself forward with the friction caught beneath my fingertips. "But you? You are childish. I knew what Robert thought of me. What he felt. What he feared. He could admit it out loud." Even in the form of a mindless, enraged rant. "But he didn't lash out and brood like a child—"

"Enough," Mischa growls as I reach for the rim of the tub. "Stop this. You've made your point."

He advances and shuts the water off. Then he grabs my waist and positions me upright by the water's edge.

"I understand now. You have the bastard whipped." He fishes the rag from the tub, but when he brings it to my skin, I slap his hand away. When he tries a second time, I swipe at his arm, knocking the rag from his grip. A low, ragged inhale is my warning of his annoyance.

But pain is the only antidote to fear.

"I said don't touch me."

"Then wash your fucking self!" He snatches the rag and throws it at me.

I flinch as it slaps against my hip, but then I grab it and dip it into the water myself.

"While you're at it, get yourself back into fucking bed as well."

"I will." Crawling to my room seems impossible—at least until I look him in the eye. I'll do it. Even if I have to use my fucking teeth for leverage. "I'd rather break every damn bone in my body than rely on you for anything."

His mouth quirks again and my stomach clenches in response. "Do it," he goads. "I'll even bring you a fucking hammer. Then you'll just remain my captive forever."

"Captive?" A nasty, broken sound rips from me and I barely recognize it. A laugh? I try smothering it beneath my palm, but it's too late. I force my trembling fingers to my side and meet his gaze head-on. "I thought you said I wasn't? Or is liar a term I should add to the list of differences between you and Robert?"

When he says nothing, I gamble my little bit of pride on two snarled words: "Get out!"

He shouldn't leave so easily. Not without putting up a fight or biting out one final insult. Regardless, the door slams behind him and I'm alone.

Which would be a welcome fact in any other context but this. Mischa fits the dog comparison well; he only retreats in order to plan an even more vicious assault.

Still, I swallow hard and pick up the rag, washing myself as best as I can. He left clean bandages for my chest, which I don't have a hope of tightening, as well as a fresh, plain cotton nightgown. After cleaning myself as much as possible, I pull the nightgown on.

And now what?

I eye the door and brace my trembling fingers over the marble flooring. I'll crawl. I will. Determined, I start to shift my weight, pushing off with my palms, moving toward the door inch by inch.

It flies open when I've barely made it a foot away from the tub.

"Here." Mischa shoves something into the room that clatters over the floor.

I cringe as it comes close, only to blink as my brain struggles to register the bulky shape. It's black and small, rolling with its own weight. A wheelchair?

"So you say you don't want to be a captive?" Mischa echoes. He grabs me by my waist and hauls me into the wheelchair. "Then come. And earn your fucking right to call yourself anything else."

My heart pounds as I watch him leave for the umpteenth time. I want to ignore him. Ram myself into him. Scream. Shout.

Anything but follow. As a compromise, I delay the inevitable by sinking back into the chair. With both hands, I ease my casted foot into the closer leg rest and gingerly maneuver the other the same way. My fingers drift to the wheels on either side, testing them. With moderate effort, I maneuver myself from the bathroom and into the hall.

Mischa's there waiting. Without a glance in my direction, he starts down the hall. To his office. I recognize the wide study beyond the doorway.

"You want to talk business, Robert's wife?" He's behind me in an instant and quickly wheeling me toward the desk.

Alarmed, I throw my hands out to brace myself against the wood, but he pulls me to a stop at a safe distance.

It feels so strange to be out of bed. Despite knowing that he has yet another game in store, I can't smother a sigh of relief. His office is a new dungeon at least. A new battlefield.

"So talk to me, partner," Mischa says mockingly. "Tell me something amusing. Maybe…" He taps his chin as if he's thinking, but there's something on his mind. The reason behind his hostility maybe?

I'm caught off guard by how desperately a part of me wants that to be the case. At least we can finally get it out into the goddamn open.

Then he says, "Maybe you can tell me why Sergei Vasilev stopped asking for you?"

"What?" It takes everything I have to school my face into a blank mask. "What are you talking about?" At least the confusion in my voice sounds genuine. The last time I saw the wizened rival to my captor, he gave me a necklace. One still around my throat now, though I don't dare reach for it.

"Don't play dumb." Mischa circles to the opposite end of the desk and leans against it, bracing his palms flat over the surface. "The old man is planning something and you are in the center of it, I bet. I noticed his sudden change of heart *before* your little accident."

Yet he said nothing. Why? He turns away, denying me the chance to discern anything from his expression. His posture is just as inscrutable.

"Did you speak to him?" he wonders. "Or maybe you made a deal? He'd treat you to a nicer cage if you traded yourself in return. Was he the one who served you up to Nikolaus—"

"Why are you so concerned about me and other men?" I find myself blurting. "Even my husband wasn't that possessive."

It's a lie, but Mischa chuckles nonetheless. "Possessive? Oh, no, Little Rose. I'm on my guard."

The look in his eye chills me to the core.

Licking my lips, I risk asking, "What could I possibly do to you?"

The answer is obvious without him having to say it: nothing.

Right now, I couldn't even slap him if I wanted. Already, I'm doubting that I'll have the strength necessary to return to my room without his help.

Lost in self-pity, I almost miss his genuine chuckle.

"What could you do?" His eyes narrow and focus inward at something only he can see. Finally, he grits his teeth. "A woman like you can do more damage alone than a thousand Robert Winthorps. Do you want to know how?" He pauses for a second before answering himself. "Because you can sneak into someone's fucking head and twist it. You play them like little puppets. Don't you?"

Denying him would only set him off. I can see it, the anger lying in wait, anticipating the second I'll light the fuse. With Robert, I'd know exactly what role to play and what words to say.

With Mischa? I can only act on instinct and hope for the best.

"I want to ask you something," I tell him. "And if you answer me honestly, I'll forget how you've insulted me. I won't mention Robert again and I swear that I'll respect whatever boundaries you set—"

"And there you go," Mischa growls. "Trying to get inside my fucking head!"

"A question," I say calmly in the wake of his shouts. "Just one. What did I do to make you so goddamn angry? Do you even know?"

His nostrils flare as he pushes back from the desk. Deliberately, his hands flex in and out of fists, and I tense in anticipation of his next move. To hit me?

"Why? *You*," he finally admits. He approaches me and flicks his finger along my jaw once he's close enough. "You made me so goddamn angry—"

"Tell me why." I bite back another phrase. *Use your big words.* It's what Mother would sternly encourage Briar during the worst of her tantrums. *Speak. Explain.* "Just say it!"

"Fine." He frowns, still stroking alongside my chin. "Did you mean it?" There's no anger in his voice. Just cold curiosity.

"Mean what?"

"Those things you said to Nikolaus. About me."

"W-what?" I rack my brain, fighting to remember. "Oh," I rasp as my own boasts come back to haunt me: *You are half the man Mischa is.* Fire floods my cheeks as I recall the other things I said—to save my life. Did I mean them? "I…"

"And there you go." He sinks down into a crouch and grips my chin, forcing me to face him directly. "Playing your mind games again."

"And what if I did?" I say. "What if I meant them?"

His mocking sneer falls flat, and he stands, withdrawing his hand. "Then I'd know you really were a goddamn liar."

"And you?" Consequences aside, I reach out, grasping his forearm. To my surprise, he doesn't wrench away. Yet. "For all your talk of hating me and how fucking awful I am, why do you even care? Are you jealous of him? Of Robert?"

He laughs. "Oh, Little Rose. I wouldn't get any cute ideas. I would be wary of you even if you weren't his wife." His tone is too smug.

Experience warns me not to challenge him. The words are already out of my mouth regardless. "Why then?"

"Why?" He brings his face close to mine, inhaling my scent. "Because of who your mother is, Little Rose. I've heard the stories… But I'm not allowed to mention her, am I?"

I can't disguise the pain constricting my face. Satisfied, he turns away, another battle won.

"Wait." Fighting back tears, I fix my gaze on him as he stops paces from the door. "I can't make it back to my room alone," I admit. "And you can hold your grudge if you want and insult me if that soothes whatever pride of yours you think I damaged—"

His lips spring apart, but I keep talking.

"Just know that I'm too tired to hate you. In fact, I don't hate you. And I refuse to be your punching bag."

He grinds his teeth, smothering whatever words are fighting to escape his throat. Or perhaps he's chewing on them, ensuring each one is loaded with lethal, biting candor.

"You don't hate me, huh? So then why do you flinch every fucking time I touch you? In the bath," he adds as my eyebrows furrow. Then he puffs up confidently, ready to challenge a lie or excuse.

I recall my shock at how he maneuvered the rag, and the confession spills from me before I can censor it. "I...I didn't expect you to be gentle."

Faced with the truth, he deflates, frowning. I don't know how long we stay like that, watching each other in silence.

Mischa senses someone approaching first. He's already standing by the desk, his arms crossed, when one of his men enters the room.

"Pakhan, I..." The man trails off, spotting me.

"You can speak," Mischa commands. "What is it?"

The man casts me another furtive glance but then sighs before clearing his throat. "You wanted to know if anyone might oppose you at the next gathering after what happened with Nikolaus?"

Mischa tilts his head at full attention. "And?"

"Your position seems solid. Nearly everyone responded to our inquiries with full support—"

"Good," Mischa says, nodding.

"But…" The man rocks back and forth on his heels. "Gabriel Medvedev and Sergei Vasilev haven't responded. Yet."

"Oh?" Something icy flits across Mischa's gaze. "Now I know why Vanya sent you in his place."

"Pakhan—"

"Enough," Mischa snaps. "Inquire again, and this time, you come to *me* directly with their answers. Especially Sergei's."

The man nods and races off.

"And you…" Mischa addresses me, his eyes downcast. He rubs his chin, thinking. "You really want to prove your worth to me?"

"And I haven't already?"

He seems to mull it over. Then he shakes his head. Apparently, I haven't.

"What do you want?" I demand.

"You," he says simply. The candor in his tone makes my body deflate of anger. "I want your loyalty, Little Rose. Are you willing to stand beside me if I ask you to?"

He's deliberately vague—not that it makes a difference. In his world, I have few options but him.

Or Sergei.

I fight to school my expression as I consider the possibility for even a second. Would I dare trust a man I don't know? A man whose only tie to me is through a woman who I'm beginning to realize I never understood at all?

It takes me just seconds to settle on an answer.

"I don't have a choice."

Mischa cocks an eyebrow, but for once, I sense that he's more intrigued than angered. "Oh, but you do, Little Rose. You know you do. But I don't want your answer now. In fact, I don't think I want you to say a damn thing. I want you to show me."

"How?"

Movement from the corner of my eye reveals that he's circling around to my end. His breath strikes the nape of my neck as my wheelchair jolts forward. Moments later, we're back in the room with my designated sick bed.

I eye the sheets as Mischa brings me up to the mattress. He pulls them down and a familiar scent irritates my nostrils. Lavender. When he starts to slide his hand beneath my waist, I stop him, gripping his forearm.

"I'm not tired," I croak. It's a more dignified way of saying what I can't out loud: *Don't make me stay here again.*

"Suit yourself." He releases the wheelchair and heads for the door. "Have your run of the house, Little Rose. *Walk* the grounds to your heart's content. I have nothing to hide."

The boast would sound more convincing if it weren't for the harshness in his voice.

A man like him *lives* to hide and obfuscate.

After all, what is a monster without his secrets?

CHAPTER 16

"*Have your run of the house.*"

What I first interpreted as a cruel joke turns out to be far more nuanced once I inch my way into the hall, alternating arms to wheel myself along. Things I never noticed before take on a newer context. Like how, despite the obvious age of the manor, the rooms sport newer doors, slightly wider than most. Or at least I assume so given how easy I can maneuver my chair through them.

Aljona. Perhaps, after all this time, I've finally learned the real name of the woman haunting Mischa. Not Anna-Natalia, but his sister. A twin.

They left her there, twisted in the wreckage.

Was this chair hers once upon a time?

I wander aimlessly, creeping down the hall at a snail's pace, hunting for clues from a new perspective. I wonder if her room was the red one. Perhaps those clothes were hers. The perfume. The red bed with its heavy canopy.

No. Mischa would hide her memory somewhere more sacred than that. Perhaps down this hall I can't remember venturing in before? The soft carpet cushions the wheels of the chair and I only have to use half the effort. At random, I stop beside a door and open it.

I don't find a bedroom at the other end—or a figurative crypt. Instead, a section of the floor pitches gradually into shadow. Almost like a stairwell, but devoid of steps. Without thinking, I run my hand along the nearest wall, finding a light switch.

Orange light illuminates what could be a wooden slide that curves toward the interior of the house.

My throat goes dry as I ease myself along the curving path. It's no longer than the servant's staircase at Winthorp Manor. Within seconds, I'm on the lower level of the house. Back near the dining room, I suspect.

So Mischa wasn't lying about having a sister.

The reality of that fact stuns me, leaving me motionless in a shadowed section of the hall. All the things he said take on a new context. The pain in his voice. More than that: the skill and care with which he cleaned me. Cared for me.

And maybe now I know the real reason as to why he was so angry with me. Ironically enough, I doubt even he knows the answer. At its core, it's the same reason why Robert Sr. hated me.

I'm not his sister. If anything, I'm just a stark, painful reminder that she's gone.

And what he's become.

A monster.

A murderer.

My tormentor.

Lost in thought, I maneuver myself backward and escape up the ramp. Minutes later, I'm back inside the white room, and I risk injuring myself again just to crawl onto the mattress. It isn't long before Vanya delivers another meal.

When he's gone, I wait, somehow knowing what's in store before I even hear the heavy footsteps thud against the floor. When he appears in the doorway, he looks more ragged than he did earlier. His hair has been scraped into a messy knot on the top of his head, his jaw lined in a five-o'clock shadow. With little fanfare, he strips his shirt in the darkness but leaves his jeans on as he advances on the bed.

"I know you're awake, Little Rose," he calls to me. "I can smell you there, fucking festering in your haughty little pride. You got pretty far, even hobbled. Maybe I'll take the chair? Make you crawl? I'd love to see you always on your knees…"

I stiffen beneath the sheets. Did he sense me there in the hallway after all? But no. He sounds more callous than vengeful. Aggravated. Once again, something has him itching for a fight.

And a part of me feels exhausted enough to give him one. Let him play his silly game.

"Tell me about your sister," I demand, lunging for the one topic that I suspect affects him the most. "What was she like?"

He stops in his tracks, impossible to read in the shadow. "My sister?" he echoes thickly. "She was better than *you*."

"You never mentioned her before," I point out, ignoring his insult. "Why? You talked about your mother. Anna. Never her."

My skin prickles, and I can imagine his expression: eyes narrowed, spitting fire.

"Maybe you aren't worthy enough to hear her fucking name?" he challenges.

But there's more to it than that. It's in the pain lurking in his voice. The gritted, grated undertone to every word.

"How did she die?"

"Oh, Little Rose…" He laughs that cruel, callous laugh and my stomach sinks. I've gone too far. "Do you think you can handle the gory details? Are you that hungry to hear tales of your husband's crimes?"

Of Robert? No. My tongue flits across my lower lip in a futile bid for silence. I want to say nothing. "You said she had your soul," I blurt out instead.

"Oh?" The mattress jolts as Mischa lowers himself onto it, sitting with his back toward me. His shape flickers, followed by a heavy thud. He's taking off his boots. "Do you think I'll cry if I relay her pain to you? You want to feel sympathy for me, the monster of your precious fucking fairytale with Robert Winthorp?"

"I want to understand you." My cheeks flame at the confession, but it's too late to take it back. Sighing, I continue. "Vanya said that you used to be different—no. I *know* you used to be different."

Sixteen years ago, he saved my life. Even if he didn't realize just who I was at the time. For the first time in ages, I let myself picture him as he must have been then. His face was softer. His posture was lighter. His sister was still alive, I suspect.

"She died, Little Rose," Mischa says, his tone cold and final. "It doesn't matter how. All that matters is the why: Your family took her away from me—"

"You're not the only one who lost someone to the Winthorps."

Oh, God no. My fingers fly to my lips as if to seal the confession away. But it's too late.

Like a shark sensing fresh blood, Mischa cocks his head. His arm sweeps out and the fingers aim for my stomach. "You mean *this*," he says without elaborating. It's like the bastard is in my head, sensing the thoughts I've locked away, even from myself. "Tell me."

"No."

His hand presses more firmly, as if he can crush the answers from me. "Why?"

"Because…" I close my eyes as the truth escapes me once again. "Because I don't trust you. I don't trust you not to use it against me—and I will *die* if you use this against me."

"Die," he scoffs. Then the bed shifts as he lies back, stretching his legs out before him, but he says nothing as he thinks. "You think I care about what upsets you?"

I'm prepared for his mocking, but his voice lacks the hostility I'm used to. Instantly, my guard rises. "I think you care about very few things."

"You're wrong."

I jump as my hair is disturbed. He's taken a lock of it, twisting it around his fingers.

"I don't care about a damn thing."

"That's a sad way to live," I say, my voice rasping.

"Is it?" His voice is louder, murmured near my ear. "And what about you, Robert's wife? What do you care about in that tiny, shriveled heart of yours? Him?"

I sigh, suddenly exhausted. Years of suffering Robert's games have never drained me like a few minutes with Mischa does.

"I want to know why you are the way you are," I tell him. "I want to know what makes you tick. I want to know why a man like you is so afraid of seeming like anything less than a heartless monster. Even for a second."

"And I want to know why a woman like you would sell your soul to Robert Winthorp." He grips my chin, wrenching my head in his direction.

In the dark, he looks more demonic than human. All I can make out are his eyes. Flashing, fiery embers.

"I want to know why that same woman would give herself to me. Why sometimes she looks at me like I'm her fucking dog and she owns my leash." He yanks me closer and his breath on my neck burns me. Consumes me. "I want to know why she moans my name when I'm inside her and whispers *his* in her sleep. I want to know why she's in my head. Inside my fucking skin."

He slithers over me, bracing his weight on either side of my head while his torso hovers above mine. His mouth is a furnace, scorching the skin of my neck, each word like a flame. "I want to know why she plays her games with me. Toys with me. Am I that much of a fucking animal to her?" Then he lifts a hand from the bed to grasp my chin, forcing me to meet his gaze when I try to turn away. "That much of a fucking fool…"

He lowers his face to my neck. Sharp pinching pain makes me gasp and flinch into the sheets. He bit me.

"I want her to answer me," he growls into my skin. "I want her to fucking admit it. Come clean. You want to seduce me. None of it is fucking real—"

All I have to cling to are his own words. "It's just sex."

"*No.*" He rears back, hunched like a predator ready to pounce. "It stopped being sex when you said those fucking words to Nikolaus. It stopped being sex that night in the fucking hotel. From the moment I first touched you, it stopped being sex." His hand slips between my legs, plunging beneath my thin nightgown.

I cringe, my cheeks flaming. I should feel disgust. Weak and at his mercy, I should feel helpless.

Not senseless.

One touch and I forget. This room. This place. His fucking twisted insanity. One touch and he's inside me, and he feels so different from Robert…

"You fucking see?" he hisses, snapping my attention back to him. "This is what you do. You pretend and you trick, and —" He breaks off, his teeth clanging as he shoves a finger inside me. I barely hear him above the moan that rips from me. "And you make me fucking think for a second that I could have you."

He sounds crazed. Obsessed. Insane. His voice deepens in ways I've never heard, not even at the heights of his rage.

"You're praying to go back to him, aren't you?" he wonders, still stroking me from the inside out. "Not that it fucking matters. I'm inside you, Ellen Winthorp. I'll always be inside you…"

There are no words to describe what he does to me. It's a torturous style of fucking I've never been subjected to, not even at Robert's most sadistic. Fingers, rubbing… everywhere. Igniting me. My hips writhe, desperate to stifle the flame he ignites. Chase. Evade. Anything to feel more. Feel less.

He's ruthless, wringing something from me I never thought was possible before him. A high and a fall so mind-blowing that all I can do is wheeze, and pant, and suffer.

His hand is still between my legs when I come back down, punishing me with slow, deliberate flicks of his thumb.

"Tell me what your game is," he murmurs, but there's no anger in his voice. Just a naked, terrifying plea. "Tell me. Just fucking admit it. Say it. Tell me!"

His teeth snag my lip—hard. I choke a cry against his tongue, and his lips move harshly, capturing the sound. His tongue does to my mouth what his fingers did to my body. Capture. Control. Claim. But unlike with Robert, he doesn't want to smother me. Each ruthless, hungry pass strokes something in me, like blowing on a smoking bit of wood. Within seconds, it's blazing with no end in sight.

"You want to drive me insane," he suspects against my quivering lips. "You want to. Like him. But I'll take you down with me, *Elle*." He nips again, drawing blood. I swear he does. At the same time, he smooths over the wound with a laving stroke and all pain dissipates. "I'll make you crave me just as fucking much. I'll burn you down to the ground and there won't be anything left for him to steal back."

We're fused, mouth to mouth. Soul to soul—and it's so easy to let him swallow me whole. His fingers return between my legs, stroking and teasing, but never hard enough. Fast enough. He's always an echo of what I know he can be.

"Not tonight," he whispers, finally drawing back. "Not tomorrow. Not the day after, but soon. When I've decided to put you out of your fucking misery. When I've had enough of playing your game—because don't you forget for a second: I've always been playing your game."

He stands, but he doesn't leave. Not right away. He stalks to the other side of the room instead. I see him there, a shadow flung against the wall, slinking and blending into the darkness. He moves into a corner and takes up a post there, watching me well into the night.

CHAPTER 17

I shouldn't have been able to sleep. Nonetheless, I come to on my side, blinking in the harsh light of dawn. At first glance, I assume Mischa's gone: I don't see him nearby.

Then I feel it. Warm breath on the nape of my neck. At the same moment, I sense the slight pressure over my waist, just enough to avoid jostling my injured ribs.

He isn't awake. I realize that the second I flinch and he doesn't issue a mocking taunt. He groans instead and the mattress shifts as he withdraws his arm—only to fully turn toward me, releasing a heavy sigh.

He smells strange like this. There's no vodka. No musk of hate. Just the heady scent of his breath tainting the air. Watching him, I subconsciously tally up all the differences between him and the figure I know him as most often, stricken with rage. The lines of his face are softer now. He looks younger.

He looks…tired. Like someone who's lived a long, hard life and deserves every ounce of sleep to be found. But the second I let myself think as much, his eyes fly open and he's transformed. So much of his appearance hinges on his mouth. Flattened in the peacefulness of sleep, he's almost beautiful. Hardened and cautious, he's an enigma, impossible to decipher.

Especially in silence.

Without a word, he stands and redresses in the clothes he left on the floor overnight. Then he turns to me and rips the sheets from my body. I'm in his arms with no warning, forced to cling to him during the trek into the bathroom.

After he sets me on the bench, I watch him run the water and gather his supplies with clinical precision. His focus makes it harder to reconcile the harsher, violent pieces with a man capable of unfurling a roll of bandages and lining up a row of soft rags to clean me with.

Perhaps talking to him is the only way to shatter the awkward thoughts going to war in my head. "The little girl Nicolai gave you…" I cringe at my own word choice, though I'm not sure how else to phrase it. "Does she have a name?"

Mischa stiffens, still crouched, his head bowed. "Why the fuck would I know or give a shit about something like that?"

I swallow hard at the grit in his tone. He's not bluffing—or so I would believe if I hadn't seen for myself the different side of him. A man who can braid a child's hair and teach her how to hold a knife. In some alternate universe, I assume the act would be equivalent to showing someone how to ride a bike. Parental.

"Because I saw you with her," I admit.

Predictably, he stiffens, his gaze shooting up to mine. His eyes narrow and I can see the word aching to leave his tongue: *snake.*

"You were good with her. Do you have children?"

Given his lack of protection with me—the wife of his sworn enemy—I have no doubt that a child must have come into play at some point. His quick smile, however, is too feral. Only now do I realize that I've opened myself up to his new favorite line of attack.

"Do you?"

I turn away, blinking rapidly. "Why you and not Vanya?" I ask, changing the subject to one even more lethal. He simply can't resist the bait: the mentioning of another man. "Why did you care for me?"

"You'd like that, wouldn't you, Little Rose?" His hand captures my chin, forcing me to face him. He observes me closely, nodding as if finding the answer to a puzzling question in my expression. "You would. You're a tough woman to crack, I will give you that." His fingers curl, stroking along my jaw, raising goosebumps. "But you are easy to read too. Too easy. I just have to know where to look. And it's this..." His finger creeps down to my collar, brushing my throat with a teasing swipe. "I've decided that this is how I'll break you."

"How?" I rasp as air sticks to the inside of my lungs. A complication from my injuries? No. It's him, poisoning every breath I take, invading my bloodstream in place of oxygen.

"With warmth. With that gentleness you fucking crave so much." He stands and cinches the hem of my nightgown in his fist. Then he raises it, forcing me to lift my arms or get caught in the motion.

My cheeks flame as I watch the fabric hit the floor. His scrutiny is a razor, slicing through my thin resistance.

Maybe he's right. I don't know how to protect against him when he's like this. But I'm quickly learning how exactly to fight back.

"How many women have you had?" I wonder, my voice rasping. Licking my lips, I try again, willing my tone to be stronger. "A wife? A mistress? Someone like you..." I trail off pointedly, surprised by just how wild my imagination runs. I can see them all. Tall women. Thin women. Empty, moldable, breakable women. "I'm sure you have a harem somewhere."

"A harem." He seems to taste the word and then grunts, dissatisfied. "Weak men surround themselves with scores of easy whores," he says. "Just as weaker men surround themselves with one—"

"So a wife, then," I assume, curious despite myself. A wife, with a mistress or two on the side. "Where is she?"

"Who says I have one?"

He sounds so smug. Damn it. I've misread him again. Going off his voice alone is too risky—I have no choice but to chance observing him directly. He's standing before the tub, his expression confident. But something in his eyes draws my attention. A hostile, defensive gleam.

"You don't have a wife," I say. "You don't keep a woman at all."

It's a strange way to put it, downright misogynistic. A man keeping a woman—but that's how Robert saw it. In a way, maybe that's all love really is. Beautiful, polished ownership.

But it's a role Mischa hasn't undertaken. Why?

Women flock to him, I'm sure of it. Women like the desperate maids of Winthorp Manor who hunted Robert's men—or, in some cases, my husband himself. They liked the thrill of playing with dangerous, damaged men. Some of them entertained fantasies of fixing them.

Most quickly learned the folly of that hope.

"You don't share your bed with anyone," I add, furthering my suspicions. Yet he has no qualms with doing so—he's certainty haunted mine. Could he simply be a lonely man, unable to attract the opposite sex? No. There's more to it. Hell, it might be the most obvious explanation of all. "You don't trust anyone. Not to say you trust me," I add in a rush, "but I'm under your control. I can't leave. There is no real risk in using me."

"If only that were the case," he says quietly. "But there is more to you than meets the eye, isn't there, *Ellen*?"

"Maybe there is." The words are out before I can take them back. Perhaps there is no point in resisting him. He frowns at my change in tactic, wary. "I give up. You're right. Everything I do is a ploy to seduce you."

Even admitting as much, apparently.

He cocks his head to the side, suspicious. "Do you really think you can?"

I remember that I'm naked as his gaze rakes over me. Suddenly, he stoops to lift a rag from the floor. Then he switches the water on, making it hot enough that steam forms as it pours into the tub. In silence, we wait as the water level rises. From the corner of my eye, I catch the moment he finally comes for me, rag in hand.

He lifts me sideways, sliding one arm around behind my waist and the other beneath my legs. My arms automatically go around his shoulders, tightening as he steps down into the tub, still fully clothed. He sets me on the floor and wraps my cast in plastic. Then he turns me to face him, muscling into the space between my legs.

"You're shivering, Little Rose," he scolds as he wets the rag with one hand and glides it along my shoulders. "One might think you're afraid."

"I'm not." I sound so tired. So…bored. A man who's tormented me for weeks is bathing my limbs with all the care of a nursemaid and I don't care. But I do. There's something unsettling about him when he's up this close—in a way more than just fear.

I think I can see it now, what Vanya does. Mischa isn't evil. He just smothers whatever strives to do good inside him. It's obvious in how his fingers twitch as he washes my arms and then my torso. It takes effort on his part to resist the urge and gingerly cleanse my every bruise and scrape without rousing pain. He *wants* to rub and scrape and hurt—I can see that.

Humanity is a battle for him, one he has to fight tooth and nail.

I'm not sure how much time passes before he finishes. Hours? Minutes? When he finally lets the water drain out, he dresses me in a plain nightgown and returns me to the wheelchair.

"I want to know something," I blurt as I watch him pick up his supplies. "You said you're the leader of your *mafiya*—"

"*The mafiya*," he corrects.

"How?"

He isn't terribly young, but he's definitely not the oldest of the men I saw at his last gathering, either. Vanya alone possesses his own quiet strength and wisdom that would make him a suitable leader in his own right. And Sergei. For whatever reason, the other man stood aside for Mischa.

Why?

"You certainly ask a lot of questions."

"You promised to enlighten me," I point out. "I want to know."

More than that. I want to know why a man like him can amass seemingly so much power and yet have so little. Robert pined and scraped in the shadow of his father for years, but one might think he ruled the whole world because his arrogance was so unmatched.

"Should I tell you a story, Little Rose?" he wonders as he tosses the soiled rags into a hamper. "About how a stupid, young prick worked his ass off to earn the right to be a fucking king? In your world, power is handed to those who are born with it stamped on their asses by virtue of whose dick they sprang from. But in mine…" He runs a hand over his arm, drawing back a sleeve to reveal a hint of the patchwork of tattoos adorning it. "In mine, it is paid for in blood and politics. I am where I am because I bled for it and clawed for every piece of it."

"So tell me how," I hear myself rasp. I sound genuinely curious despite myself. Maybe a little desperate as well. I could keep comparing him to Robert—but there's no point. Every tool of survival I honed until now is rendered useless in this realm and against this monster. I have to relinquish all of my old, pathetic habits. I need to study this man from the ground up.

Starting with anything he'll give me.

"I… I'm listening."

He frowns, cocking his head. "Are you now?"

I stiffen as he advances, only to watch on in confusion when he brushes past me and enters the hall. He lingers near the doorway, a silent command for me to follow. My heart races as I trail him down the hall and toward his infamous study. Once we're both inside it, he closes the door and I hear him lock it.

Purely to intimidate.

"Come here." He approaches his desk and snatches something from an open drawer. A notebook, the one he wrote my recollection of Robert's accounts in. Beside it, he places a pen, and then he looks up, finding me still near the door. "I suggest you take notes."

He leans back with his hips braced against the desk and addresses me from over his shoulder. "Where should I start? Oh, I know. You women are so drawn to sentimental bullshit. My father was Sergei Vasilev's right-hand man, and from the moment I was born, he informed me that I would never succeed him. I was too weak, you see. And, like a fool, I thought that was a *good* thing."

My fingers graze the wheels of my chair, inching me closer despite the tension in my gut warning me to flee.

"I thought he was ruthless. Brutal. That he would rather fight than fucking listen. I used to think that made *him* weak. But now I know…" His eyes flicker toward me, meeting my gaze. "He knew what it takes to survive, Little

Rose. Your husband's father killed him personally. Put a bullet right between his eyes." He taps his temple. "But even then, I could ignore their petty war. What is that saying? You live by the sword, you die by the sword. But my mother? My sister? No. They lived by flowers, and ponies and goddamn sunshine. They didn't deserve to die like animals, but it didn't make a difference in the end, did it? Life isn't fair, Little Rose. Men like your husband get to die peacefully in their beds, surrounded by their fucking spawn, while those they torment and terrorize suffer. So why shouldn't they also suffer?" Suddenly, he tilts his head back, facing me again. "I thought I told you to take notes."

I reach for the pen, forcing the nib against the notebook's page.

"There are ten families," Mischa explains. "Though each member isn't necessarily related by blood. They designate loyalties. Each leader is responsible for running a different aspect of the syndicate. We are not like your husband's family, who uses virtual slave labor and money to sway politics to their favor. We put in the hard work to run our empire."

"Your father was one of the leaders?" I ask.

"One. He managed the business aspect but wasn't strong enough to lead. He deferred to Sergei."

Again, his voice holds the same mixture of fear and respect that taints it whenever he refers to the former leader.

"Sergei led the *mafiya* from the time he was twenty," he continues. "He was fearless and branched out into new territory. He was the one who stood against the Winthorps when they became too bold. He used their own ruthless tactics against them—"

"And," I add, my voice shaking, "he took my mother."

Mischa nods. "That was just the beginning."

"So why did he step down?"

Misha shrugs again. "I don't know." He sounds annoyed by that fact. "One day, he just did. The only way someone can be named the Pakhan is with a majority vote by the other leaders. When I bid for the right, Sergei put his weight behind me."

"But you don't trust him?"

"I trust *Ivan*," he says. "His support is all I need. But should I lose it…" He turns, bracing his hands flat over the desk. Hunched forward, he looks like a wolf readying to pounce on its chosen prey. "He's drawn to you," he admits. "I'd be damned if I knew why. But know this: I won't let you poison him against me."

He's not joking. He really believes I could. Is his paranoia that great? Or is he that worried about what he's become? Or not. Maybe he simply knows that, at some point, Vanya simply won't follow him anymore.

He starts to say something else, but a knock on the door draws his attention. "What is it?" he demands.

One of his men enters the room—I guess the door wasn't locked after all.

"Sir, you wanted me to tell you when Sergei responded?"

Mischa nods. "And?"

"Well, he requested a meeting. Tonight."

Mischa frowns, his brow furrowed. "A meeting? With who?"

"You," the man replies. "And…" His gaze cuts nervously in my direction. "Her. He mentioned her by name."

"Did he now?" Mischa's eyes narrow into slits. "Tell him I'll accept, but on my terms. Go."

The man leaves, taking most of the air in the room with him.

Without even looking in his direction, I can sense the vicious verbal tirade brewing under Mischa's skin. The hate. The jealousy. I could wait and brace for the tempest.

Or I can sigh and head him off with a dare of my own. "You said you wanted my trust?"

He says nothing. Because he's brooding, I find when I look up. A wild mop of golden hair obscures his eyes as if he raked his fingers through it.

"Take me to the meeting," I propose. "Let me talk to Sergei on my own, and then you tell me why I shouldn't trust him. Let me decide on my own who to believe."

"And why should I?" There's no coldness in his tone, for once.

"You told me I should stop acting like a doll," I remind him. "So don't treat me like one. I can think for myself—"

"Fine." He rises to his full height and moves to the door. Wrenching it open, he addresses me without looking back. "I'll let you gamble, Little Rose. Let's see just what you're willing to bet."

He's gone in seconds, and alone, I listen to the thud of his retreating footsteps. My heart races, tracking the time with every frantic beat. What the hell was I thinking?

The answer is simple. Nothing. For once, I wasn't thinking —I was surviving the only way that seems possible where Mischa is concerned. Pure, volatile instinct.

CHAPTER 18

He finds me in my room when night falls. Dangling from one of his hands is a black dress, which he has to help me into. Then, still without word, he seizes my chair from behind and wheels me into the hall.

We don't take the ramp. He brings me to the top of the staircase instead and then lifts me from the chair entirely. Startled, I cling to him as he brusquely carries me down the stairs and through a corridor I recognize as the one leading to the large meeting room he held his last gathering in.

This time, a table has replaced the circular arrangement of chairs, and only one man is seated.

Sergei's aged at least ten years since I saw him last. More gray streaks his hair, and lines surround his mouth, etched into the skin. When he sees me, he stands abruptly, his expression constricted. "I heard about the...incident with

Nikolaus," he states as Mischa approaches. His side of the table contains two chairs, one of which Mischa shoves me onto.

But he doesn't rush to claim the one beside me. Instead, he extends his hand, his gaze guarded. "Sergei."

"Mischa." The other man clasps his hand in return, shaking it. "I thought it was about time we talked."

"So talk," Misha commands. He's being rude.

I'm not well versed in their hierarchy, but I can suspect from Sergei's raised eyebrow that he's caught off guard. Still, he disguises his alarm well.

"I want you to reconsider your options," he says. "By now, you know what the boy is capable of. He'll retaliate. The girl will be safer with me."

"So this is what this is about…" Mischa laughs, shaking his head. Then his hand moves so fast that I almost miss it. In a flash, he yanks a knife from his pocket and has the blade against my throat.

"Stop!" Sergei nearly lunges across the table as the metal grazes my skin. "What are you doing?"

"Something I should have done a long time ago," Misha replies. He presses the knife harder, drawing a gasp from my throat. It's not for show. Sharp, pinching pain alludes to the fact that he's already sliced through skin. "What is she to you? Enough fucking games. Just come out and say it."

"Let her go." Sergei's eyes move from my captor to me, flashing with uncertainty. "Mischa—"

"Fucking say it!" The knife withdraws as he slams the blade onto the table so hard that the legs shudder. "Now. So she can hear you. Is she yours? Is that it?" When the other man doesn't answer, he points the knife at me again. "I fucking swear to god—"

"Remember who you are talking to."

I jump at the authority ringing in Sergei's tone. He's transformed in an instant, and now, I see that Mischa was right to be wary of him. "You show me respect, boy."

"And you show respect to me!" As Mischa grabs me from behind, his hand forming a collar around my throat, a gasp rips from me. "Tell me who the fuck she is. Tell me now."

Sergei's gaze flickers beyond us to the doorway. "Mischa…"

"I said tell me! Is she your fucking bastard—"

"I think she's *Ivan's* bastard!"

Silence descends so abruptly that every breath I take echoes tenfold, deafeningly loud. Mischa's gone from my side, standing paces away. "How?" he demands.

"How else?" Sergei shrugs. "Her mother was Marnie Winthorp, wasn't she?" When he doesn't receive an answer, he nods anyway. "She was. Ivan may seem grizzled now, but don't be fooled. He's younger than I am, always too damn soft for his own good. And to be honest…" He trails off, eyeing his hands. "I thought I'd erased any threat that woman could pose to him years ago. In fact, I'm surprised my brother hasn't already deduced her identity for himself—"

"He hasn't because she's not," Mischa snarls. I turn to face him, standing paces away, his eyes fiery. "Her mother was a fucking Winthorp whore. She's no more Vasilev than the dirt on the bottom of my fucking shoe."

"And if you were lying to me, you know that alone would give me enough of a claim to challenge you." Though he and Mischa are the same height, Sergei suddenly seems larger, exuding a confidence he lacked before. "Because if she is of my blood, you know what that means."

"Do I?" Mischa counters.

"It means my bloodline would have life in it, Mischa," he replies, his tone deadly soft. "It means I'd have an heir to my name. And it means that perhaps I wouldn't be so content to sit back and watch the next time your carelessness puts my people in danger."

He eyes me pointedly, as if demanding I come clean now. Admit it.

"Do not get me wrong," the man adds, returning his attention to Mischa. "I do not want to challenge you. But if I feel that you may have insulted and battered my family? If I feel that my bloodline is in play once more? *If* I sense that you are more of a threat than a true leader…" He lets the unspoken threat hang in the air. "For now, continue your war with Winthorp if you have to. You still have my support. But think carefully about where you lead from here. And let me know if she happens to remember anything that may clear up her paternity."

He leaves, carrying himself with that dangerously subtle aura.

And Mischa waits, reminding me of a child ensuring that the adults are out of earshot before resuming his bullying of those weaker. "Don't tell me you believe him? He's a feeble-minded old fool—"

"You knew." My voice clashes with his, a weak whisper against a shout. Surprisingly, mine wins out. "All this time…and you *knew*."

His face blurs as my eyes well over and tears spill down with no hope of suppressing them. Everything he said flashes through my mind. His jealousy. His paranoia.

And Vanya…

His kindness. His gentleness. Did *he* know? The answer sits like a stone in the pit of my stomach. No. He didn't.

"Did you get a sick kick out of it?" I snarl, surprised when he flinches. "Watching him care for me? Holding my life over his head? Did you love teasing me about my mother when all along you knew!"

"And that is why," Mischa says softly. "Why you shouldn't believe everything you fucking hear. Don't entertain your childish little fantasies because the reality isn't what you want it to be—trust me on that."

He could be mocking me again. I wish to God he were, but for a rare, stark moment, he's being honest. I can see it in his face, the hints of pain that only slipped out when he talked about his sister.

"Vanya treats you kindly now, but that's because you're a nameless victim. An innocent. But if he knew the truth? Not only would he hate you, but the pity. The disgust. Bitch at me all you want, but trust that I know what it is like to be shunned by your own father. It's a pain I wouldn't wish on anyone."

"And I'm supposed to believe you?" I croak. "You don't give a damn about me. If I'm his niece, Sergei has a reason to want his throne back, doesn't he?"

His jaw clenches over an answer, but he doesn't have to say a damn thing out loud.

"You're a selfish bastard. God, I hate you—no, I pity you. Now I see why Vanya sticks around. It's not because he knows you can change—he doesn't. He's just waiting for the moment he'll have to put you down like the mad dog you are!"

I blush at my own vitriol. I've never spoken like this to anyone. Not Robert. Not Briar. In a sick, twisted way, it feels so damn good. At the same time…

Mischa's face reveals nothing but a careful, blank mask— and I'd prefer any other reaction.

Without a word, he turns, leaving the room, his posture relaxed.

But hatred is like a boomerang. I feel the aftereffects strike me long after he's gone, lancing across my chest in an unexpected manifestation.

Guilt.

CHAPTER 19

I don't return to my room. Instead, I crawl into a corner and sleep in a chair, tucked away in some distant corner of the house. Maybe I do it out of spite, shunning what few items of comfort he's provided.

Maybe it's shame.

In some ways, it helped to believe that my father was some faceless, nameless monster. Even when I thought he was Sergei. Those possibilities were men I didn't know, whose kindness and mercy I couldn't recall. Had my parentage been more sinister, it would hurt but I could handle it.

I can't handle this.

The lies, and the intrigue, and the secrets. Vanya wasn't always the man he is now, Mischa warned me once. If Sergei really is right, could I reconcile that horrible monster with the man who treated me with more kindness than a majority of the people in my life?

And Mischa…

I hate him. At the same time, I know it's pointless too. You can't blame a dog for biting and howling when it's all he knows. You can't expect a monster to feel an ounce of goddamn mercy.

So I don't. Gritting my teeth, I focus on the only person I have control over in the situation. The only fool I can blame. Myself.

Alone in the silence of a forgotten hall, I contemplate every fucking mistake I've made up until this point—trusting Mischa even for a second is one of them. My fingers absently trace the fresh scratch he left over my throat. Did he goad Sergei intentionally?

Or did he mean in every word of his threat to kill me?

I should believe so. I should fester over it—another reason to hate him. Loathe him. Despise him. He's a childish bastard with no fucking soul, but that's the catch.

Children are never malicious without reason. They're defensive, like Briar all the many times she made me submit to her. At his core, Mischa is an insecure, immature bastard. But there's a reason behind his madness, and I can't shake the sinking suspicion that he lied to me, and to Vanya, for a reason.

What exactly that may be?

I don't care.

I *can't*.

If I stay hidden, I can almost pretend I'm back at Winthorp Manor, a realm I know well. Robert would give me a day or so of peace, just long enough to recharge my soul and lick my wounds. He'd never have to hunt for me because I'd instinctively know when to return to my cage and wait for him. I was a well-trained bird.

I'd never listen to heavy, thudding footsteps I knew to be his pacing the hallway nearby. My new captor never calls for me out loud. He can smell that I'm close. Sense that I'm near.

Overall, he has too much damn pride to surrender.

So we play our silent game for hours. His footsteps retreat. Return. Retreat again. I think it's hours before a door finally opens, revealing the creature standing behind it. He's dressed in black from head to toe, his hair a stark contrast over his pale skin. Shrouded by a wild fringe, his eyes glow —intense, but not angry. Beside him is the wheelchair.

For what feels like an eternity, we eye each other until he finally moves, turning his back to me. His hand shoots out, shoving the wheelchair further into the room. "The doctor is here," he growls, his voice hoarse.

I watch him go. Only long after his final steps trail off do I move. Mischa isn't waiting for me in the hallway or by the main stairs. Alone, I find the ramp and maneuver myself to the second floor. Inside the white room, I find a strange man wearing a white coat.

An hour later, my cast is in pieces and the doctor props a pair of crutches against the bed.

"Practice bearing weight gradually," he warns. "I'm going to recommend that Mischa allow a physical therapist to come."

With that, he leaves, and I attempt to stand only to cling to the bed frame with white-knuckled hands. The crutches are harder to maneuver with than the wheelchair and I can only move a few feet at a time. Sweat dribbles down my neck by the time someone enters the room to witness my struggle.

"Careful!" Vanya races to set down a tray of food. His arm goes around my shoulders, providing enough stability to keep me from pitching over. Then he steers me to the bed, murmuring the whole time. "Do you want to fall and break another bone?"

It's too much. His voice, the soft, gentle cadence. His touch. My head is spinning and I clutch it beneath my fingers as if stroking my temples can unravel the tangled thoughts. "I'm fine. Just please... I-I need to be alone."

"Are you all right?" His fingers still over my shoulder, but I don't look up to see his reaction.

"I...I'm just tired," I force myself to reply. "I just need sleep."

"Get some rest. I'll leave the food here for you." He pats me gently and then leaves, and the dam of emotion I didn't even know I was holding back breaks loose.

I manage to smother the first sobs beneath my palm. Eventually, that isn't enough. A handful of bedsheets. A pillow. Only by biting down over my palm can I stay silent in the end.

My eyes stream as my body heaves. There's no comparison for this pain. I just have to suffer through it, experiencing every emotion I've ever felt tenfold. Agony. Guilt. Relief. Gratitude.

It doesn't last long. The second I hear someone approach, I choke my sobs down and fight to compose myself. Not Mischa. I'm aware that my newcomer isn't him even before I face them from over my shoulder. This figure is smaller. Thinner. Her blond hair is a wild, matted tangle, clashing with the blue, feminine dress someone gave her to wear.

She eyes me from partially behind the doorway.

"Can I help you?" I rasp when she doesn't move.

She shakes her head. Then she points to the tray near my bed and mimes eating with her hands.

"Mischa," I snarl. Once again, the bastard proves that he isn't above sending a child to do his dirty work.

"I'm not hungry," I reply politely, hoping my irritation doesn't seep into my voice. "I'll eat later…"

I trail off as she pads closer and lifts a bowl from the tray. Holding it out to me, she nods to the broth within. Apparently, I have no choice.

It's a thin, simple soup but still delicious. I drain it quickly under the girl's watchful eye. Satisfied, she starts to leave the moment I swallow the last drop.

"Wait," I call out, and she pauses near the doorway, impatiently fidgeting with the skirt of her dress. "What's your name?"

Her wide eyes meet mine and she shrugs.

"You can't talk?"

She shrugs again and then scurries away before I can ask her something else. This time, however, I follow her. It takes me ages using the crutches—or so it feels like. By the time I enter the hallway, I only have the sound of her quick steps rounding the corner to guide me. It isn't long before I can get a sense of where she's headed. Sure enough, not far from Mischa's office, his voice greets me.

"Did you do it?" he demands gruffly. "She ate all of it?"

The girl must nod or whisper something to him, because he grunts, satisfied.

"Fine. Here's your share."

I come close enough to make out the smaller shape of the girl standing before the desk. Mischa must place something onto her hand, because she draws it back, observing the contents intently. Then she extends the same hand toward him again.

"Good," the man praises, slapping something else onto her palm. More money, I suspect. "Never trust anyone not to

cheat you. Always count your shit. You catch on quick—"
Suddenly, he cocks his head and a frown distorts his mouth.
"But next time, I will teach you how to ensure that you
aren't followed."

The girl whirls around, spotting me.

"Go," Mischa tells her.

She whizzes past me, and I attempt to follow her.

"Wait."

I don't want to. Every cell in my body is screaming at me to
keep moving. Ignore him. Resist. I manipulate one of the
crutches forward and take a step.

"I said to fucking wait."

Old Ellen Winthorp would have obeyed the twisted
baritone. She would have cowered and let him inside her
head again. New Ellen, however, is too fucking tired. I keep
inching along as my neck prickles with an awareness of the
man glaring after me.

He doesn't follow me though. I reach my room alone and
collapse, panting, onto the bed. Here, I curl up and try once
again to process everything swirling around my head
without going insane. When I hear the soft steps of
someone approaching, I don't try to be polite.

"I'm sorry, Vanya, but I'm not hungry—"

"Look at me."

I guessed wrong. My body stiffens at the sound of Mischa's voice.

I lift my head just enough to spit out, "I'm not in the mood to be used as a fucking pawn in your goddamn war, either."

He stands there so long that I'm sure he'll attack. Lash out. Insult. I'd like to think I'm ready for him, but I'm not. I'm so tired of his game.

Closing my eyes, I lie here with my face buried in the sheets. I'm not sure exactly when he leaves. The only thing I'm aware of is that darkness falls gradually, confining me like a cocoon.

And that he's gone.

CHAPTER 20

*H*e doesn't come for me in the morning—or if he does, I don't give him the chance to. I hobble to the bathroom myself and bathe behind a locked door. For clothing, I settle on one of the items I picked out for myself what feels like an eternity ago: a dark sweater and a loose pair of jeans.

A part of me wants to stay in here forever. Hide from the monsters in my life. Pretend I have any say in doing so. Lie to myself. Is that how my mother survived her days? The more I think of her, the less clearly I can recall her memory. Not the sweet, smiling woman who tucked me into bed some nights, but a haunted shadow. Someone with more secrets than answers, and even now, I'm not sure I want to learn them all.

Eventually, the heat of the bath water fades and I have no choice but to escape into the hall, using my crutches for balance. Out here, I realize that Mischa might be the least of my worries. Something in the air is different: a sense, a feeling. It permeates the narrow hallway, seeping through my skin. Unease? Just a few paces from the bathroom, my ears catch the distant sounds of men talking. Furiously.

"What do you mean?" a man demands. Mischa. "You think they're here? Would the bastard really be so fucking bold?"

"What is your gut telling you?" someone replies gruffly. Vanya. "Something isn't right—"

"It's Winthorp," Mischa hisses. "He's planning something. Or maybe Sergei… Fuck these goddamn games!"

"Well then what are you going to do about it?"

I hear them both move farther into the house, splintering off in different directions. Vanya's slow, uneven gait heads away from me, while the other set…

I watch him ascend the stairs dressed in gray fatigues, his hair wild and untamed. His eyes find mine, dark with an unreadable emotion. Without a word, he cocks his head, beckoning me to follow him into a nearby room. His office.

My heart beats unsteadily, and I start to turn away.

"We need to talk." The grit in his voice draws my attention despite everything. He's wary about something. Me?

He's seated behind the desk when I finally enter the room, his hands braced flat over the surface.

"You're coming with me tonight." He looks up, seeking out my gaze. "I'm meeting someone with information on your husband. You say you're truly free of him? Prove it to me—"

"Why should I?" I counter, my voice soft. "Why should I believe anything you say?"

"You don't." He pushes back from the desk and stands. "But use your brain, Little Rose. You want information on your husband? Your mother?"

He lets the question hang in the air like a tempting piece of bait.

"Then be ready tonight." He wants to say something else, I suspect. His lips twitch and then twist into that stubborn frown. Without another word, he leaves, retreating down the hall.

My heart clenches with an emotion I can't name. More confusion? The man delivers it in spades, like a poison meant to affect me when all of his other attempts have failed. All I can do to survive the effects of it is…

Breathe.

I inhale raggedly between every step I take. At first, I head for my room, but something makes me pass it and turn the corner to that forgotten wing. I test the doors one by one, surprised to find most of them locked. The few that aren't open onto dark, dusty closets that contain nothing of real interest.

Mischa guards his secrets well, it seems. Well enough that I'm exhausted by the time I return to my designated sick room—not that I can enjoy the peaceful quiet for long.

He comes at the time when Vanya would usually bring my evening meal, his steps hesitant near the threshold. With the door already opened, I can make out the sliver of his shadow outstretched over the floor. He says nothing, and I have to rise from the bed and approach him to convey my intent.

His eyes narrow, and then he turns, leading the way to the lower level. To my surprise, he takes me to the stairs, forcing me to hobble down and balance my crutches while clinging to the banister. Dripping sweat, I watch him, trying to decipher his motive. To punish me?

No. His arms twitch at his sides as if he's stopping himself from offering assistance. Maybe because he knows I'll rebuff his attempts—regardless, he stays close. Close enough to catch me should I fall…

His eyes, however, reveal nothing as they track my descent, and the moment I'm close enough, he marches for the door, leaving me to follow. Two of his men wait outside near an idling van. One takes the driver's seat, while the other climbs into the farthest row at the back of the van, which leaves me and Mischa to claim the middle.

Mischa makes me get in first and snatches the crutches once I'm seated. To my alarm, he leaves them there on the driveway before climbing in himself and slamming the door after us.

"What are you doing?" I croak.

"You won't need them." He stares from the window on his end, his posture tense.

Alarm dances down my spine in deadly anticipation. Very few things make Mischa pensive—none of them good for me.

Are we headed toward another meeting? Another dark, sordid trade? Perhaps, even now, he still plans to sell me, a task made much easier if I don't have full use of my legs.

The twisted scenarios form unabated in my head. My breath is baited by the time the vehicle finally slows to a stop. When I look out the window, all I feel is…

Confusion. "Where are we?" The question slips out before I can remind myself who I'm with.

We're near a secluded building. A home maybe? It's not as grand as Nicolai, the drug supplier's, but it's not small, either. It's perhaps the size of the guest house at Winthorp Manor. In the darkness, I can make out two men standing guard on a short set of stone steps leading to a door. Orange light illuminates square windows, but I can't make out any hint of what might lurk within.

"Get out." Mischa shoulders the door open on his end and renders his command moot when he reaches for me. Before I can protest, I'm in his arms. "Don't worry, Little Rose," he grunts as he heads for the front of the building. "I'll release you soon enough."

The reassurance rings more like a threat as we near the two men who eye me warily before nodding in deference to Mischa.

One of them opens the door, allowing us inside. A narrow foyer decorated in shades of black and gold greets us, a much chicer interior than I would have expected. Mischa enters boldly and turns through a nearby archway, entering a wide, simple sitting room. A man dominates a leather couch in one corner of the room. I stiffen the second his eyes connect with mine.

I don't even register grabbing Mischa's forearm until he shrugs, testing my grip. "What—"

"He was there with Nikolaus," I say. "The night he attacked me."

"Pakhan," the man greets, his tone soft. "How kind of you to join me."

"It seems you've been busy, Gabriel," Mischa replies. He sets me down on an armchair positioned slightly beyond the circle of couches. Turning his back to me, he claims a seat directly opposite the other man. At a glance, I can't tell if he believed me or not, but then—as if he read my mind—his hand goes to the bulging pocket of his fatigues. "Care to explain yourself?"

"Can you blame me for assisting an old friend?"

"Maybe… *If* you have the information you promised," Mischa counters, "I suggest you make it good."

"Yes…" The man shifts, unfurling his long limbs. He places his hands on either knee, and a ring on his left hand draws my eye. Thick. Silver. It looks similar to a Winthorp insignia ring, but different. Older. "You've been busy yourself, Mischa," the man says. "But Robert Winthorp? Well, he's been busier."

"Cut to the chase, Gabriel," Mischa scoffs, crossing his arms. Then his eyes cut in my direction before flicking away. "I'm listening."

"He's consolidating," Gabriel declares. "Everything that bastard could inherit from his father, he's already pried from the man's cold, dead hands. The docks. The ports. All of it."

My skin runs cold at the mention of Robert. Still alive. Still fighting back. Without his father, I can only imagine how far the depths of his greed might extend.

"I'm not worried about the Winthorps and their toys," Mischa says.

"Ha!" Gabriel throws back his head for a guttural laugh. When he meets Mischa's gaze again, he isn't smiling. "You should be. With the power at his control, he could crush you in a matter of weeks. With or without the *mafiya*. And if he's bold enough to come after you directly, all it would be is catching you off guard. Not to mention your little rift with Sergei…"

"A matter of weeks, you say?" Mischa strokes his chin, seemingly unconcerned—but I can see through the act. His eyes are molten, swirling with dark conspiracies.

"He's been busy, Pakhan. Making alliances. Scurrying in your shadow. You think you have a good grip on your men. Maybe you do—but don't doubt for a second that Winthorp isn't in the background, sniffing around for any hint of weakness. If I could plant a man among your ranks, just imagine what he could do?"

Interest crosses Mischa's expression. "So what do you suggest?"

Gabriel eyes me again, a slight smile shaping his lips. "Well, if you had some *insight* into who his allies are, that might help."

"That's what you're for, if you haven't forgotten," Mischa says coldly. "Unless I need to find another man whose palms require grease. Preferably one who won't scurry around with my fucking enemies—"

"Relax, Pakhan. Nikolaus was a cousin of mine, you understand." His gaze turns distant for a brief second. Then he shakes his head. "Rumor has it that Winthorp's moves are a bit too bold. He's more confident than he's ever been, but why? Or maybe it's self-preservation. His father had several businessmen who might think they have a claim to what the old man left behind. Robert's consolidating power quickly. They might be willing to whisper to any man who could guarantee their safety."

"And I assume you have someone in mind?" Mischa wonders.

"That I do. I'll pass on his information to you, but there's more."

"Oh?"

Gabriel nods, suddenly serious. "There are more rumors, a bit more outlandish, but I think you might want to consider them nonetheless. One is regarding Winthorp's sister. Her wedding's been mysteriously called off. The whereabouts of her fiancé are unknown—"

I must have made a noise, because the man breaks off, turning his attention to me.

"Some say it's coincidence," the man continues, "but I say that the bastard is getting rid of any threats to his power, even his own blood."

Mischa shrugs, disinterested "What else?"

"Another rumor. This one is…more gossip than anything, but it might serve your purpose if it pans out. There is talk that Winthorp wouldn't cut off his own sister and attack his father without securing his own bloodline. His father was a madman, you realize? Had it specified in his will the exact stipulations of any inheritance."

I remember them. Archaic nonsense Robert used to scoff at. He could only marry someone his father approved of and produce a male heir. One of the many reasons our relationship wasn't valid in the eyes of his father.

Briar's wedding, in terms of succession, put her one step closer to securing the elder Winthorp's favor.

"You know how some of those old-fashioned fucks loyal to that family are," Gabriel sneers. "They've all supported him, but they wouldn't without proof that he's established himself as the head of the Winthorp name. Dogs need their rewards, you see."

"Proof?" Mischa sits forward, an eyebrow raised. "What kind of proof?"

Gabriel shrugs. "The kind that would make a man bold enough to imprison his sister—allegedly—and kill his father. There's talk that he had a pet he kept close." Once again, his dark eyes dart in my direction.

This time, Mischa copies him and my heart stalls at the intensity of his gaze.

"And?" my tormentor prompts.

Gabriel's lips quirk into yet another quick smile. "*And* there's talk that he may have cemented his bloodline, if you know what I mean."

I stop listening. My stomach churns ominously, even though I know it's a lie. I *know.* But the knowledge swirls in my blood like poison, making it harder and harder to breathe…

"I need fresh air."

Both men turn in my direction as I rise from my chair, using the arms for balance.

"Wait." Mischa advances on my position before I can even make it to my feet. Within seconds, I'm in his arms, being carried from the room. "We'll continue this later," he calls to Gabriel.

The other man merely laughs. "Of course."

Tension radiates from Mischa, seeping through my skin as we enter the cold night air. He all but shoves me into the van, climbing in after me.

"Drive," he snaps to the driver. "And get Vanya on the phone as soon as you can. The fucker's up to something. I can sense it. And you…" His eyes cut to me. Before he even opens his mouth, I beat him to the punch.

"It's not what you're thinking." Even now, I can't even force myself to say it out loud—the scenario that I know is on his mind. "It's not."

"Oh?" He laughs. "And I'm supposed to believe that because you fucking say so?"

"Yes." The simplicity of my answer makes him grunt in shock. "I wouldn't lie about this—"

"About what?" Mischa demands as his man dutifully puts the van into motion. "About your fucking spawn with Winthorp? Let me guess. *Now* is the time you beg me to spare them both—"

"There is no child." My fingers fly to my lips, suppressing the confession. It's not the whole truth. Inhaling raggedly, I try again. "They… He died."

Mischa says nothing, even as my body deflates with the admission. Hunched over, I focus my attention on breathing. In and out. Ironically, he's the one who taught me this mantra—how to survive when it feels like the world is caving in and nothing could possibly slow the onslaught.

So I breathe.

When I finally let myself refocus on my surroundings, the van has stopped. Muted noises echo as if I'm hearing them from underwater. Shouting. Mischa. We aren't near his manor, I realize, but parked along a country road. Shadows obscure any defining features and I can't even begin to guess our location.

Mischa stands outside the van, with the door on his end wide open. Carried by a harsh wind, his voice drifts to me, tense and low.

"What the fuck do you mean?" Suddenly, he breaks off, his eyes wide. "Shit!" The next second, he's lunging into the van, shouting in the driver's ear. "Drive! Fucking drive!"

The van explodes into motion, kicking up mud as it peels down the road. Soon enough, Mischa's manor appears on the horizon like a smudge of brown over an inky sky. A smudge is quickly enhanced by strokes of orange and yellow.

"No! Fuck, no!" Mischa slams his fist into the back of the seat before him as the driver swerves off the road, cutting through a field to reach the house sooner. Yards away, Mischa flings the door open and jumps out with the driver hot on his heels. "Safe house," Mischa shouts.

Gritting his teeth, the driver turns back to the road, and the sudden increase in speed jolts me forward—but he's not fast enough. A dark shadow swerves from a curve in the road up ahead. A quickly approaching van—but it's not one of Mischa's.

I only have a second to make out the blurred faces beyond the tinted glass before everything explodes into noise. I'm spinning. Falling…

Crashing.

Pain licks lazily at my throbbing limbs as I feel out with my hands, desperate to get my bearings. It's dark, barring a faint glow of moonlight that illuminates nothing in particular. But I can get my bearings, at least. I'm lying on my side, caught between the front and middle seats of the van.

"Hello?" I call out, but the driver doesn't answer. Groaning, I manage to climb to my knees only to find the man slumped over the steering wheel. I don't think he's breathing.

And then I hear them: footsteps crunching over grass and dirt, racing toward me.

The van must have stalled rather than crashed. It's still upright, and someone grunts as they wrench the door open. Blinking, I struggle to take them in. A pressed suit and gleaming headset affixed to his ear confirm the worst: He's not Mischa's.

Frowning, the man observes me. "It's her," he grunts into his headset. "I've found her. She's alive." He tucks his gun into the pocket of his coat and extends his hand. "Come with me, miss. You're safe."

Safe. Safe. Safe. That word echoes hauntingly as my ears ring and broken glass crunches under my fingertips, a painful reminder. This man will take me to Robert.

"We need to hurry!" The man stoops to my level and reaches for my arm.

Robotically, I reach out in return, letting him guide me to the door.

A hiss escapes him as he observes my legs. "She's injured," he barks into his headset. "Our location is—"

"Help me up!" I command over him.

He frowns but assists me to my feet. In the distance, Mischa's home glows, engulfed in flames, and shock renders me speechless. All those secrets I'll never uncover. The memories Mischa obviously holds dear. And the people…

Vanya. The little girl.

Mischa.

"We need to move, miss." The man beside me loops an arm around my shoulders, steering me toward the sleek, black vehicle idling paces away. He must have driven it himself. There's no one else inside as he sets me on the passenger's seat.

Faintly, I can hear shouting in the distance. Screaming.

"What's happening?" My voice comes out a dry croak.

The man shoots me an odd look and once again fidgets with his headset. "Have medical standing by," he mutters. "She's injured—"

"What's happening?" My heart races as the man takes the steering wheel. Rather than head toward the house, he turns down the road. Toward Robert.

"You're safe now, miss," he explains, his voice terse. "Mr. Winthorp decided to put an end to this little game once and for all."

That damn word—*safe*. From who? Mischa? With Robert?

"Stop the car."

"What?"

"Now!" It's like another woman is speaking, not me. One who sounds so damn cold. Determined. She sounds like Mischa. "Now!"

"Miss?" The man narrows his gaze and the van seems to move faster. We're nearing a bend in the road. One that will take us beyond Mischa's property and into the unknown. "We'll be there soon enough—"

"I said stop the car!"

I lose my mind; that's the only way to describe it. It's like my consciousness detaches from my body. I can see myself lunging for the wheel, batting the man's hands away. I can sense the vehicle swerve dangerously. Then a violent jolt as everything comes to a sudden stop.

But it isn't until I'm blinking up at an impassive night sky that I register the pain flooding my body. I taste blood. My ears ring so loudly that I can barely hear the telltale crunch of footsteps racing toward me. Something is still in my hand. Sharp. Jagged. Broken glass. Dazed and broken, I somehow manage to lift it, brushing the tip against my collar.

Do I really have what it takes? Maybe I do. Anything to avoid returning to Robert…

"Easy!" someone shouts, sounding nearby. "Easy…"

I inhale sharply at the familiar accent and try to focus my vision in the speaker's direction. "Vanya?"

"Don't speak." Darkness descends as he drapes something over me. A coat? It smells like him: musk and smoke. "Just hold on to me. Hold on to me."

"Don't get up too fast."

The warning comes as my eyes flutter open to an unfamiliar room. Tension laces my limbs, making them spring into action before I even fully regain consciousness. To run?

Maybe not.

Instead of a cell, I'm on a leather couch in a dimly lit room. Only a faint orange glow illuminates the weathered face of the man crouched beside me. Vanya. A cut on his forehead bleeds freely, and his left eye is partially shut and swelling fast.

Shock erases my panic. "What happened?" I hear myself rasp. But hazy images are already flickering across my mind. Fire. Shouting. Robert's men.

"It was an ambush," Vanya says gruffly. He rises to his feet, wincing, and starts to pace. "All I know is the goddamn house was on fire and we were being shot at like fish in a fucking barrel. I swear to god, if that bastard Medvedev—" He breaks off as if remembering I'm here.

"Where's Mischa?" A part of me steels myself for the obvious. He's dead.

"Mischa?" Vanya runs his hand across his face. "He's—"

The sound of squealing tires cuts him off, and Vanya lurches across the room to a window. I crane my neck to follow his gaze, catching the approach of a white van that skids to a stop near a rickety porch. The vehicle door flies open and Mischa jumps out, shouting.

"Ivan! Come help! Now!" His blond hair casts a shadow over his features that makes him appear years older than he is. Blood streaks his jaw, and he looks more predatory than ever. Inhuman. I barely recognize him as he turns and lifts something from the floor of the van.

Make that *someone*: a body, small and pale. The little girl.

"Mother of God." Vanya lumbers through the doorway as Mischa races toward the house. Somewhere beyond this room, a door opens, slamming against a firm surface. The floorboards shake as a stampede of men enters the room, led by a frantic Mischa.

"Move!" He lunges toward the couch, placing a small body down beside me, forcing me to my feet.

The girl. All I see is red. In her hair. On her face. Her chest.

My mouth falls open in horror. "What happened?"

"Don't just fucking stand there!" Mischa cuts his gaze to me, and the ferocity in it takes my breath away. "Help me!"

Instinct guides my motions. I sink to my knees, gritting my teeth against the pain, and reach for the nearest item I can find—a small throw pillow. Wadding it in both fists, I press it to the largest splotch of blood as my mind tries to process the culprit of such a wound.

A knife?

Gun?

I must have asked the question out loud, because Mischa shoves my hands aside, his voice like thunder.

"She was shot. Move!"

His hands tear at the girl's chest, ripping her shirt away to reveal the true extent of the wound: a gaping hole on her left shoulder, gushing blood. She's still alive. My eyes track the fluttering motion of the pulse in her throat to ensure that much. But her eyes are closed, her breathing rapid and labored.

"Help me," Mischa snaps, raking his bloodied hands through his hair. "Fuck…"

There's no time to think. Plan. Something inside me takes hold and drives me closer to his side, submitting myself to his silent command: apply pressure with a wad of cloth he fished from seemingly nowhere. The girl moans when I press down, her eyelids fluttering.

Gritting his teeth, Mischa barks an order over his shoulder to Vanya. Only after my brain tries to decipher it do I realize he spoke in another language. Russian? Whatever he said makes the older man move in between Mischa and me, forcing me farther from the chaos.

Eventually, I find myself shoved beyond the room entirely, into a hall that opens onto a narrow room containing a bed and little else.

Here, I listen to the noise seeping through the walls. More shouting. Hushed voices. A lone, plaintive, childish cry.

Then nothing. The silence stretches on for what feels like an eternity, broken only by the eerie creaking of the old wood of the house. The stench of dust and musk irritates my nostrils, betraying the fact that this dwelling hasn't been inhabited in a long time. Another safe house?

I don't find any clues giving a definitive purpose. Just darkness and empty spaces. Eventually, the sounds of footsteps retreat down the hall and my heart kicks into overdrive. Hesitant, I linger near the door, unsure if I should exit the room myself in search of answers. In the end, the choice is made for me when the door opens from the outside.

A shiver runs down my spine as Mischa advances a step, his head cocked to seek me out, his gaze piercing.

"I suppose you're happy now," he says. "Your husband wants you back so badly, he's willing to kill a child just to do it—"

"Is she okay?" I can't seem to breathe again until he finally nods.

"For now," he says, advancing another step. "Does that disappoint you?"

I flinch, gritting my teeth against an impulsive reply. It's what he wants, I realize. To fight. He wants anger and rage. He wants to feed off it. Exhausted and sore, I find that all I can do is sigh, noticing the reality of his exhaustion even his bravado can't hide.

"You're covered in blood," I croak.

It paints him. The dark splotches almost seem like a part of his skin when seen through the darkness. I can smell it: salty musk that conjures unbearable memories. My fingers twitch, grasping at the air, and I approach the bed and snatch a ratty bit of cotton from one of the pillows. Balled in my fist, the fabric serves as a makeshift cloth.

Mischa stares blankly as I approach him with the cloth held before me. Days ago, the look in his eye would have made me fall back. Maybe it's the pain that drives me forward? I'm limping, inhaling sharply every time my foot connects with the floor.

Even so, he looks worse.

"Here…" My hands shake as I swipe at his chin with the edge of my makeshift rag. Stiff with disuse, the fabric barely soaks up any of the reddish liquid. I have to scrub, and scrub, and…

"Enough!" Mischa wrenches from my grip, slapping my hand away.

"Sit down." My voice is a shallow whisper in the shadow of his, but he stiffens regardless.

"Why?" he counters. "So you can have better access to my throat, Robert's wife?"

"No." I swallow hard, clearing my throat. By some miracle, I'm still holding the cloth. "So that I can help clean the blood off of you before she wakes up and sees."

Something flashes across his gaze too quickly to identify. Shock, maybe? Like I've struck him. Perhaps I should. The boiling tension from the last few weeks feels like it's building to a fever pitch beneath my skin, tainting every bit of muscle and bone. Violence is a tempting outlet.

For me and for him.

I gasp as he grips my wrist, which forces me to take a step closer. At the last second, he turns and winds up dragging me toward the rickety mattress in the corner. It expels a cloud of dust as he sits, flooding the already still air.

"Before she wakes up," he parrots, tugging me even closer. "But will she? Not if your husband has any say in that—"

"I would never want to see the death of a child," I snap, tugging my arm away.

"Is that so?" His voice. He sounds too damn smug.

Here and now, I can't overlook yet another childish jab at my past. Not again. "You want to know?" Exasperated, I pose the question without thinking it through, and my heart pounds as if in protest. *No, no, no.* "Fine," I rasp, despite myself. "I did have a baby. But he—"

It's like rocks lodge in my throat, formed from years of suppression. I don't revisit these memories. Not even as every other vivid horror echoes on an endless loop. Never this. Maybe it's the one way I've followed completely in Marnie's footsteps: Some things are easier to ignore.

Closing my eyes, I inhale deeply, fighting for the strength. I can't think. Only speak. "Robert wanted the baby, at first."

It feels strange to say so out loud. Despite his overbearing possession and meticulous planning of our life together, the one-time reality shattered his façade, he welcomed it.

"I think he thought it was a benefit to him." The cold, detached woman speaking sounds like me. At the same time, I feel as much a listener as Mischa: spellbound by a story that sounds so foreign. Like it happened to someone else. "I didn't—I was... I didn't want him. Not right away."

I had nightmares, in fact. Of a tiny female or male Robert with soulless eyes. Horrible, terrible nightmares.

"But then... I started to feel him." My hand flutters to my stomach, chasing that phantom sensation. It's so real to me, even now. A strong, insistent pressure, like reassurance. There was a chance that whatever was growing inside me could turn out to be just like Robert. But it was a chance. He deserved that chance.

"My feelings changed. I think that's when he started to resent it."

I recall the slow, deliberate increases in Robert's coldness to me. The searching looks he'd cast my way. The narrowed, suspicious glances whenever he noticed me standing as I am now, with my fingers ghosting my belly.

"It's crazy... But I noticed that my meals would decrease in size. He took more maids—practically paraded them in front of me. He made—" I break off, brushing my fingers along my lips. Why? It could be the silence lingering in the wake of my confession. I don't think he's ever let me talk like this before—uninhibited, without a single cruel interruption.

"What happened next?" he prods, but his voice lacks the venom I'm used to.

"Robert got angry. I had an...*accident*, and he was stillborn," I croak. "They took him away before I could even hold him. See him. I never got the chance..."

I shake my head and lock the images away before they can descend.

"I've never spoken about it before."

Mischa is silent for so long that I think he's satisfied. Finally, he makes a low sound in his throat as if he just solved a tricky puzzle.

"Robert. It was *his* name you call out in your sleep," he deduces. "Not—"

"Yes." A dry swallow pushes the rest of the memories back. Turning to Mischa, I find him watching me, his expression more unreadable than ever. "Call me a bitch, or a whore, or Robert's fucking wife—that's fine. But don't you dare for a second insinuate that I don't know what pain feels like."

Fire sears across my vision. I'm blinking too rapidly to see. Just blurred smears of light and shadow. Swiping at my eyes with the back of my hand, I start toward where I guess the door to be.

"Wait."

Shock lances through me as he snatches my arm and tugs me backward. Why? So he can rub my nose in more agony?

"Here," he grunts, and I jump as he presses something rough against my palm.

My trembling fingers struggle to identify it: coarse, gritty, bloodstained fabric, I realize looking down. While I'm caught by his grip, he forces me to unfurl the rag and lift it to his jaw.

Up this close, there's no telling just who the blood belongs to. The girl? Him? Another? There's just so damn much of it. I can taste the salt on my tongue, cloying there like so many spilled secrets and dark memories.

Grunting, Mischa presses my hand to his cheek, issuing a silent command. *Clean me up.*

I watch my hand contort and move seemingly on its own, rubbing ineffectively at the drying substance. He'll need water and soap if he wants to make a real difference. Still, he makes me rub and scrub until he's only symbolically clean.

To him, maybe that's enough.

CHAPTER 22

I don't know how I fall asleep. Or where, exactly…

Blinking, I let my exhausted brain piece together various clues like a faulty jigsaw puzzle. A looming ceiling. Dark, wooden floors. A dust-covered blanket shrouding my sore, aching limbs. I force my fingers to curl, grasping the edge of the stiff cotton. Vanya did it, his kindness striking once again.

Telling myself that is the only way to keep my heartbeat steady enough for me to deduce the rest of my surroundings. I'm sitting directly on the hardwood floor. In a corner? A quick glance around reveals shadow broken by strips of yellow sunlight streaming in through boarded-up windows. The safe house. I recall that much.

Among other things.

Like the man looming above me, standing so tall that he nearly blots out everything else.

"Get up." He sounds rough, but I can't tell if it's due to exhaustion or rage. He changed during the few hours I slept, exchanging his fatigues for a pair of dark pants and a gray shirt. His arms are bared beneath quartered sleeves, and in the dim lighting, his tattoos resemble tendrils of darkness attempting to swallow him whole.

Cautiously, I rise to my feet, clinging to the wall for balance. I slept in the same room he cornered me in, tucked into a space across from the bed. Through the doorway, I can make out the couch in the other room. Did they move the girl during the night?

"Look at me." Mischa stops short of actually touching me, though his hand parts the air between us, ghosting the length of my jaw.

"Is the girl okay?" I ask, ignoring the part of me aching to flinch. Cower. Run.

"For now." He cuts his eyes to the doorway. "She's alive. But you and I need to talk about something else, Little Rose." Two heavy steps bring him closer to the door, allowing him to easily slam it shut. Turning to face me, he rakes his gaze along my body, his eyes narrowing over what he finds. "You really want me to believe that little sob story you told?"

I blink, more shocked than angry. Deep down, I'm not really surprised. Expect a monster to reason? Only a fool would be so naïve.

"Of course not," I spit back. "That might require some human compassion—"

Rugged fingers capture the back of my hand and the rest of my insult dies on my tongue.

"Compassion?" he wonders, tracing the line of a vein up my wrist.

Paralyzed by disgust, I can only watch, hating the feel of his skin on mine. "Let me go."

"Let's not play any more games." Something in his voice draws my interest. It's deeper than before. Tired. As if he stayed up all night, mulling this potential conversation over in his head. "No more lies. No more pretty word games. You give me what I want, and I will give you what you want."

My throat goes dry. Tentatively, I flick my tongue along my lips. "And what do I want?"

He cocks his head back, and of all things to shape his mouth, this new expression is the most alarming yet. A dangerous, half-moon shaped smirk that conveys more than the malice I'm used to. It's resigned. As if he's confident that whatever he's about to ask me to do, I'll refuse. And he's counting on it.

"You want revenge, Little Rose," he tells me. "Though I doubt you even realize—no." He shakes his head, suddenly stern. "Don't argue just yet. You want revenge on your husband, and I can give you that and more."

"But what do you want?" I demand, overlooking his assertion—for now. "You have his accounts. His secrets. I've told you everything I know—"

"And that's the problem." The intensity in his voice makes my heartbeat stutter to nothing more than a thready pulse.

He's closer, leaning in to bring his mouth near my ear. His stench assaults me, heavy and ripe. I don't think he's bathed since last night and it shows: blood and musk.

"I've drained your little skull dry, but it's not *your* head I'm after." Two of his fingers stab at my tangled hair, working their way through the matted strands. "It's his. I want to know what makes him tick, Rose. I want to know the little secrets and fucking fears even you aren't privy to. He thinks he can take me on? Well, I'm going to destroy that motherfucker from the *inside* out."

The stress he puts on *inside*…

My cheeks flame and I step back, wrenching out of his reach. "So you think the key to 'knowing' Robert is sleeping with me?"

"No." He frowns as if insulted and advances a step, heedless of how it blocks me in—though maybe that's his real motive in the end. His fingers return to my hair, parting the strands and testing the weight of a lock against his palm.

My chest tightens as I watch him. I half expect him to smell it, some primal action that would make more sense than what he actually does. He twists the stringy locks. Pets them.

"You are the key to that motherfucker," he declares after a moment. "Inside you. That's how I'll destroy him."

"You're insane." I croak, attempting to turn away.

"No." He tugs on my hair, forcing me to face him again. "I'm impatient, Little Rose. As I said before, give me what I want and I'll let you have a little taste of the one thing you've convinced yourself all along that you didn't crave."

"And what is that?"

His teeth flash. "Power."

"Really?" A mocking laugh sticks in my throat. "*You* crave power."

"Bullshit," Mischa counters. "You want it, all right. You just don't know how to fucking reach out and take it. But I can show you—"

"Oh?" I fail at bravado; my voice is a dry rasp. "And how will you do that?"

He smirks, and this time, the expression unnerves me even more. "I'll put some right in the palm of your greedy, fucking hands."

He eyes the hands in question, still grinning. Then, all at once, his mouth falls flat as footsteps approach and the door opens from the other side.

"Mischa," Vanya calls, his expression wary. "You were right. Winthorp has his men staked out for at least ten miles in either direction. He's blocking us in."

"Good." Mischa shrugs and passes him to enter the adjoining room, where a tiny body lies bundled on the couch.

The girl. I don't think I breathe until I notice her chest rise and fall with labored breaths. She's alive.

"He's planning another attack—but he'll try to isolate her first. So let him think he's won," Mischa suggests to Vanya. "In fact…" He turns to me, a mocking half smile on his lips. "I'll even let him get a taste of his prize."

"How?" Vanya wonders.

"Wait ten minutes and then lead the men west," Mischa says. Then he grabs my arm and drags me through a door that opens onto a narrow porch. One of the vans is parked nearby and he shoves me toward it before returning inside the house.

Seconds later, a low cry draws my attention to the doorway. Bundled in Mischa's arms is the girl, so pale that she practically glows in the faint sunlight.

"What are you doing?" I've stepped toward him without realizing it, my hands outstretched as if I mean to grab the girl from him.

Raising an eyebrow, Mischa descends the steps, barreling past me. "I'd concern yourself with what *you* are doing, Robert's wife," he grunts as he shoulders open the door to the back of the van and gingerly sets the girl on the farthest back seat. Crouching beside her, he looks at me and jerks his chin to the driver's seat. "She needs a doctor, and *you* are going to get her safely to one. Drive."

Icy shock paralyzes me. "You're insane," I croak.

"Yeah." He nods. "That's how I've fucking survived this long, Little Rose. Now, get in the fucking van—"

"No." I'm already backing away, shaking my head. "I can't drive."

Something crosses his face too quickly to track. Shock?

"Well, today, you're going to learn."

My heart stops as he lunges from the van and I'm reminded of just how big he really is: a towering hulk of sinew and muscle. He grabs my shoulder and steers me to the driver's seat only to shove me onto it.

"Gas," he grunts, pointing to a metal knob jutting above the floor. "Brake." He points to another knob beside the first. "Just keep us on the fucking road."

He slams the door after me only to climb into the seat directly behind mine.

"Now, drive." His breath bastes the back of my neck like a furnace, impossible to ignore. "And," he adds, "if you think of stopping to pay your husband a little visit, think again."

A hard surface nudges the back of my skull, a warning.

"Now, go."

"H-how?" My shaking fingers can barely grip the steering wheel.

"Turn it on," Mischa prompts, his tone oddly patient for once. "Like this." Reaching over me, he twists a key already in the ignition and the van roars to life.

From there, I manage to pull onto a narrow country road just beyond the driveway without prompting. If he's surprised, he says nothing.

But that distracting pressure is never withdrawn. I'm forced to contend with the silent threat it conveys while struggling to make sense of our surroundings—desolate, empty wilderness and a lone gravel road. Just where are we?

And where exactly is he taking us now?

"Why me?" I ask without taking my eyes off the road. We're traveling at a snail's pace, and Mischa nudges my shoulder in another silent command: go faster. Warily, I press the gas only to slam on the brake a second later as the van jerks forward. "Why aren't you driving?" I rasp, hunched over the wheel, my heart racing.

"Why?" He sighs like he's thinking over his answer. Then he scoffs. "Use that brain of yours, Little Rose." Again, he taps my skull with that threatening, heavy object. "Take a guess. Who do you think is watching you right now?"

"Robert?" I risk taking my eyes from the road long enough to scan the desolate fields and copse of trees beyond us. A second's appraisal reveals nothing. No long-lost husband lurking in the bushes. None of Robert's men, either.

"Don't be so naïve," Mischa hisses into my ear as if reading my mind. "He's not hiding in a tree, Little Rose. But he is watching. Yes." He inhales as if sensing the fear wafting from my skin. "And you know it—"

"I could have left the other night, you know…" I swallow hard as his eyes cut in my direction. I'm not sure why I'm confessing this now. "One of his men found me. I could have left."

"So why didn't you?"

"I don't know." I try to look at him directly, but that pressure on my skull grows.

"Look at the road," he snaps as I swerve to stay on the thin strip of gravel. "Let's just hope your husband keeps his distance now. Go faster."

Again, I hit the gas too hard and the car jolts forward. This time when I hit the brake, a small moan comes from the back seat.

"Easy!" Mischa snaps. Suddenly, a shadow flickers from the corner of my eye and a wall of heat maneuvers into the seat beside me. "Look forward," he commands as a heavy touch lands over my thigh, guiding how much pressure I apply. "Keep going straight until I say so."

He's crouched low, trying to hide as much of his bulk as he can—which is very little. His head is near my shoulder, his gaze intent. I feel it burning through my thin clothing to scorch the flesh and bone underneath.

"Faster," he warns before applying more pressure to my thigh, sending the speed gauge even higher.

At this speed, my fingers struggle to keep the vehicle straight. It's like I'm controlling my heartbeat more than four wheels and a metal carriage—with every touch, it strains against the bounds of my control.

Though maybe Mischa isn't even the cause. For the first time, I glance at the rearview mirror and Mischa has to grab the wheel in my stead, shouting as the car careens off course.

"What the fuck is wrong with you?" he hisses.

All I can say in response is, "We're being followed."

The sight of a black van in the distance isn't what triggers the panic building in my chest. It's a feeling. A deep-seated knowledge in my bones.

With every inch the approaching van gains, a part of me squirms in grim acknowledgment.

Robert didn't send just his men this time.

"Fucking focus!" Mischa grips my chin hard enough to reinforce his presence. "When I say so, you take your hands off the wheel and slam on the gas. Don't fucking let up. You got it?"

A hard swallow robs me of speech. All I can do is nod.

"Good."

I wait, but he doesn't increase the pressure on my leg, not even as the black van drifts closer and closer…

"Not yet," he scolds when my foot twitches against the gas unprompted.

The van is still too far away to make out the figure in the driver's seat—not that I need to. Robert never drove himself; he was always surrounded by his retinue of bodyguards. But he's here. I feel it. I can taste it—the fear that chokes me whenever he's near.

Like blood and ash. I'm suffocating on both.

"Now!"

My foot extends at the exact moment I'm shoved aside, crushed against the door by Mischa's bulk. At the same time, he snatches the steering wheel, twisting it hard to the left.

Vomit crawls up my throat as the world twists and turns. Tires squeal. Another cry comes from the back seat, and above it all, a deep voice reiterates the same statement.

"It's all right. It's all right."

The reassurance isn't directed at me, but it acts as an anchor anyway. I'm grounded by the unsettling baritone as my body is flung toward an unseen destination. Whether it's a comforting presence remains to be seen.

"It's all right. It's all-fucking-right."

I don't know how long he makes me stay like that, pinned beneath him, my foot on the gas. For hours, it seems like. When he finally grunts out a command to let up, my leg is cramping.

"Switch places."

The van drifts aimlessly as he shifts his weight to shove me into the passenger's seat while he claims my place with envious dexterity. The man moves like a dancer in some ways. In others, he's like a battering ram.

Looking out the window, I can't even begin to place our surroundings. Trees loom in every direction, rendering the landscape more desolate than before. There's nothing around for miles.

Including Robert's van.

"Where are we?" I warily ask.

"Far away from your husband." Mischa's disarming half-smile returns and my stomach dips in response. "Don't look so disappointed." He frowns, turning his attention to the back seat. The next second, the van skids to a stop and he's leaping from the vehicle and climbing into the back. Craning my neck, I see what caught his attention: the girl utterly still on her back.

She isn't moving.

"Fuck!" Mischa's beside her in seconds, tugging her small body into his arms. "Don't," he snarls. His eyes are wide—crazed. I've never seen him like this. "Don't you fucking dare, Aljona. Don't you fucking dare…" He lowers his head, eyeing her chest intently. Whatever he senses makes him sigh and he sets her down. "She's alright—"

"And you care." I don't mean to sound so cold. Judgmental, even.

"Don't sound so hopeful, Little Rose," Mischa scolds as he backs out of the van. "There's still some shrapnel in her shoulder that needs to be removed. How else can I sell her without keeping her alive?"

I try not to flinch. He's baiting me, and this time, I refuse to bite.

"You called her Aljona," I point out, my throat dry. "Is that her name?"

I know it isn't.

"What?" Mischa flinches and looks away. Annoyed? "She'll live," he says instead, slamming the door to the back seat. As he returns to the driver's seat, I hear him grunt, "For now."

"And you *do* care about her." Maybe I'm needling him. Maybe I need to see his face as it hardens against that assumption. He grits his teeth, glowering at the road.

But he doesn't deny it out loud.

Not once.

A monster could be concerned for the welfare of a child— but in my world, that shouldn't be the case. Robert taught me well, after all.

Or perhaps only now can I reconcile the fact that he only ever told me lies.

"Wake up."

Someone shakes me roughly by the shoulders until I peel my eyes open. Mischa. He stares down on me, his face partially bathed in shadow.

"Come," he grunts, jerking his chin toward the open door of the van. "We need to move."

He reaches past me and gingerly grabs the girl, drawing her into his arms. Hunched over her pale body, he slips out of the van and into the night. I follow him warily, waving my hand to feel through the dark as my eyes adjust.

We've reached another deserted house, but this one isn't quite as desolate as the previous shack. Made of stone, it towers above, its silhouette illuminated by a row of windows on the bottom floor, ablaze with orange light.

We don't walk far before Mischa ushers me through a wooden door and slams it behind us.

"Vanya!" he shouts, barging past me, down a narrow hall that opens onto a wide entryway dominated by a circular staircase. "Vanya! Where the fuck are you—"

"Here!" The steps rattle as Vanya descends them. Then he stops halfway. "The doctor is ready. Bring her up."

They dash to the upper level and I'm alone. Literally. None of Mischa's men are lurking in the visible corners. I doubt there's anyone guarding the door we just entered from. If I wanted…

No. I shake my head, inhaling sharply. I *should* want to— leave. Run. Escape Mischa, and forget Robert. I'd try to make it on my own, far from the whims of spiteful men and their petty wars. I'd be free—

A high-pitched whine cuts the air and my body goes rigid. A scream? Before I even register moving, I'm halfway up the stairs, clinging to a rickety banister for balance.

This home is more spacious than the last. A long hallway stretches in a half-circle with numerous doors branching off of it. The door to one has been left open, revealing the chaotic scene within.

Mischa and Vanya have the blond girl pinned to a wide bed, one at each of her shoulders, while another figure hovers above her, a metal instrument glinting in his grasp. My heart lurches to my throat, and I start forward, unsure of whether to help or do nothing.

Her chest is bare and a circular gash in her shoulder stands out in stark contrast to her frail, pale skin.

"Keep her still," Mischa barks as the man I assume to be the doctor lowers a blade to the girl's wound. "Keep her—fuck! You!" His eyes lock onto me and narrow. "Don't just stand there. Do something!"

I jolt forward and grasp the only part of the girl within my reach. Her hand. I squeeze it as I sink to my knees beside the mattress and focus on her face. Sweat glistens on her forehead, and her eyes dart aimlessly around the room, the lids fluttering.

"It's all right," I tell her as the men continue to shout and clamor around us. "You'll be okay. It's all right."

Her eyes meet mine, wide and watering. She doesn't speak —not a single word—but I keep talking for the both of us, long after her eyes finally close.

"It's all right…"

Hours later, the doctor leaves and Mischa lifts the girl from the bloodied sheets. A square bandage on her shoulder is the only clue as to the wound lurking beneath, freshly cleaned of any shrapnel. She's unconscious, but her breathing is easier and Mischa takes care with her limp limbs, ensuring that her head is supported with every step he takes.

In the end, he doesn't go far, carrying her to the next room over. This one is smaller, containing a narrow bed with clean sheets. Drawing them back with one hand, he sets her down and covers her gently. Too gently.

Aware of me watching, he stiffens as he returns to his full height. "Have you grown tired of hiding your role as a spy for your husband?" he wonders coldly. "Good. Your boldness will make it easier to hunt you down when you finally go crawling back—"

"I told you before. I could have left." I sound so tired. The statement hanging in the air could refer to the weather for all the emotion it contains. Still, I sigh and give him a half-hearted performance of the show he seems to crave. "But if you want to lash out, I'll give you a reason. Why are you so afraid to let me see that you care about her?" I nod to the girl.

"My investment, you mean?" he counters, gesturing to her body with a wave of his hand. "I'm sure she'll fetch a good price on the black mark—"

"Enough!" I reach up, raking my fingers through my hair as if to arrange my thoughts before he can knock them off track—which seems to be his only goal.

Unnerving me.

Inhaling deeply, I meet his gaze and suppress a shiver that racks my spine. "So the monster has a soft spot for children," I say, my voice devoid of any mocking innuendo. "Why are you so against letting me see that?"

"See what?" He steps in close. His chest jars mine, knocking me off balance. When I step back, he advances, herding me into the hall. "Don't let your naïve little hopes deceive you, Rose—"

"You're right." I turn away from him. We're alone and the fact strikes me as odd. No Vanya. None of his men. Why? At least there are no witnesses. "I'm done being naïve," I continue, wringing my fingers together. "So I'll take you up on your offer. I'll give you my body—"

"Don't play." His sharp intake of breath catches me off guard.

Blinking, I scan his face, hunting through those dark eyes for any hint of the lust conveyed in that violent sound.

"Go on," he snaps, baring his teeth. "Or are mind games another trick you learned from your husband?"

"No," I admit truthfully. "He never taught me how to gamble. But he did teach me the power of bartering."

Sex for safety.

Brutality for security.

Ignorance for a lie.

"So I'm making you an offer. I'll give you my body—"

"And?" Mischa interjects. He's regained his composure already, and I force a hard swallow. "Name your fucking price."

"Fine… I want you," I tell him with a sigh. "You can 'learn' Robert through my body, but in return, you give me *you*.

You let me inside your head. You give me whatever I want to know—"

"Prove it." He encroaches on my personal space a second time, towering above, his breath on my forehead—but I don't back away.

Meeting his gaze, I swipe my tongue across my lower lip to find enough traction to voice, "How?"

He rakes his gaze down my front and jerks his head toward the end of the hall. When he moves, I'm forced to catch up, trailing in his wake like a lamb being led to slaughter.

Will I cower before his blade?

Or bare my neck for the lethal kiss?

"Strip," he commands as he shoulders yet another door open, revealing a larger room and a small bed. The mattress greets me mockingly, draped in a single crisp sheet. "Then get on the bed."

My fingers obediently fly to the fastenings of my jeans. "But first…" I scan the room, desperate to come up with my own test. In the end, I blurt out the first question to cross my mind. "The girl. What's her name?"

He hesitates. A sound catches in his throat—a cruel insult, I think. His first instinct is always to resist me. Bite. Roar. Anything to disguise the hint of weakness.

"I told you my price," I remind him. Slowly, I let my hands fall to my sides. "Unless you don't want—"

"She doesn't speak." As his breath fans the back of my throat, I jump. "So I don't know what it really is. I call her Mouse. She answers to it well enough."

"Mouse," I echo. Not bitch. Or whore. Or a mocking twist on a flower.

"Now, your turn," Mischa prompts, radiating impatience.

I picture him standing there behind me, his hands inches from my skin, ready to rip and tear into it. Then I let my eyes drift shut as I find the front of my pants and peel them open. It's surprisingly easy to tug them down my thighs and kick them off. My shirt takes more time to wind up. Maybe I'm testing him. Teasing him.

His breaths seem to grow hotter the more my skin is bared. Another low growl catches in his throat when I finally stand naked.

"Don't think you can just lie there like some sacrifice," he warns, drawing a single finger down my hip. "I need—want you to move. You moan. Don't you dare pretend like you're some martyr."

"I won't." I turn to face him, surprised by how true my voice rings out. "I don't mind having sex with you."

My cheeks sting to hear it said out loud.

"But that is all you will get from me without upholding your end of the bargain. A body. If you can't be honest with me—"

"But can you be honest with me?" He chuckles smugly, as if already aware of the answer. "It doesn't matter. You tout your body like it's a prize, but do you even know how to wield it?"

His hands fan out boldly over my hips, drawing me into him. Warm lips nudge my earlobe and I shudder. He's turned the tables already.

"You want power, Little Rose? I'll show you where it lies…"

The pad of his thumb traces a path down my belly, ghosting the flesh of my inner thigh before drifting even lower. Too low. Finger by finger, he cups me fully, forcing my legs apart. A low groan betrays his satisfaction as I resist my body's natural inclination to flinch.

"What men have killed for," he grates through clenched teeth. "Died for. And you don't even fucking know…"

All at once, he shoves me toward the bed. I throw my hands out in front of me, bracing myself over the lumpy mattress. Before I can regain my bearings, he's behind me, grasping my waist and flipping me over.

"I won't feed you the same lies he has," he tells me, sinking to his knees like a man before an altar. The altar of a despised deity he serves unwillingly.

Dark eyes flit over my naked skin, settling on my scars. My barely healed injuries. My eyes. He meets them directly, boring through me like a missile through paper.

"What lies?" I rasp when he hasn't elaborated.

He scoffs and my knees tremble as his breath scorches the flesh between them. One of his hands settles on my thigh, using it as an anchor to drag me close.

"The lies he used to keep you, Little Rose," he taunts, but the mocking smile shaping his lips falls flat. "You are beautiful. More than most women—even despite this." He gestures to my scarred limbs. "But that is not why he hunts you. Why he obsesses over you. Why, even now, the bastard is thinking of you. Dreaming of you…" A devious smile contorts his lips; he relishes that fact.

At the same time, it irritates him.

He slides his hand beneath my knee and tugs, opening me up to him further. "Ask me why," he murmurs as his gaze tracks a tortuous path down my neck, over my chest and lower… "Ask me."

Air wheezes in and out of my throat in pathetic bursts. I have to inhale deeply to find the strength to obey. "Why?"

"Because of your heart, Little Rose," he replies, sounding bitter.

Callused fingers inch along my skin, creating a numbing rhythm of sensation and friction. Up, up to my waist. Across. Down.

"Your eyes. You look at a man without the foolish hopes and dreams most women do. Or the greed." He sighs: a harsh sound between a growl and a laugh. "You look at a man…and you tempt him, Rose. You're naked and open, and you show him what he is back. Like a mirror. And some stupid men, like your husband… They believe that they can change that reflection. All they have to do is make you moan."

Wet heat explodes through my core, paralyzing me. Only vaguely do I realize what he's done as I watch his head move, crowned by wild, blond hair: use his tongue. *There.* Slowly and unhurriedly, without a goddamn care for the foreign sensations crashing through my body.

"If he can make you cry, Rose. Scream his name. Whimper." He speaks each word into me and my eyes flutter, threatening to roll. "Then he can…shape that reflection… He won't be a monster. Not anymore."

A cry chokes from my throat, drowning him out. All I can do is feel and writhe and reach for him. Push him away—I want to push him away. But my fingers disobey me, clenching through his hair, dragging him closer. Deeper. More. More more.

I'm on the brink, so close to going over the edge. One more flick of his tongue will get me there—I know it. So does he, because he draws back just as the sparks ignite and it's like dumping water onto a newborn fire.

"Like that," he tells me, his lips glistening, his eyes dark and unfocused. "You trick your men like that."

He makes it sound so evil. I tempt him. I torture him. *I'm* the one with the power, not him.

"Now…" He shoves his hands beneath me, cupping my ass, his nails drawn. "I'm going to—"

"No." I prop myself upright on my elbows and shove him off. Every movement takes twice the usual effort. It's like I'm drunk. His promise of power echoes in my head, drowning out all logic.

"Taking back your offer already?" he snarls.

"I want to taste you." Where did the words come from? I don't know. Unbidden and dirty—something I've never spoken before.

Taste. Only he makes it sound anything but degrading. It's a weapon. To learn and incapacitate your victim. To understand.

And I want to taste *him.*

His eyes narrow at the request. "I thought *your* body was the bargain?"

I can't think—so I don't. He doesn't expect me to buck free of his grip. His shock buys me seconds to slip from the mattress and grasp the front of his jeans. He stiffens like stone and it's nearly impossible to maneuver my fingers enough to undo the zipper.

"You bite me and I'll kill you," he hisses, betraying the source of his apprehension: He thinks I'll hurt him.

But when my tongue cradles the tip of him, I'm not sure what I want. Or what I'm hoping to find in his gaze as I part my lips around him. My heart pangs when he goes rigid. This is stupid. Demeaning.

But then his jaw goes slack around a hoarse gasp. His eyes widen. His head falls back, his lips parted. "Fuck…"

He breathes out with every stroke of my tongue and fists his hand through my hair.

And I feel it. Power.

His flavor explodes on my tongue, ripe and raw. His essence seeps through my skin, feeding me the secrets he won't say out loud.

Heat unexpectedly shoots through me, gathering between my legs. I'm rocking back and forth, grinding my thighs together to relieve the ache, even as he swells in my mouth, pulsing and thick.

"You think you're in charge, Rose?" He snaps his fingers to draw my attention, but I've never taken my eyes off him. "You are…" He reaches out, encircling my throat in his grasp. Then he squeezes just tight enough to tease the promise of danger. "This is what I can give you that he can't. *Control.*"

He tugs, forcing me to release him. Like a doll, he manipulates me to straddle his hips, his cock between my legs, throbbing on the brink of release.

"I can let you on top," he says with a groan as he lowers me onto him, inch by impossible inch. His mouth finds my ear as he swears, "I can let you set the pace. Take me as deep as you fucking can. I'm not afraid of you, Little Rose—not like him. I don't want a caged fucking bird." He grunts, bucking his hips as I settle against him, chest to chest, pelvis to pelvis. Our foreheads meet painfully, and his lips nudge mine, forcing them apart. "I want a woman," he says, snarling each word, forcing me to choke them down. "A woman who knows what she wants. Who knows which man can make her scream…"

My vision blurs as he rocks into me. Hard at first. Then unbearably slow. The greater the friction, the more weightless I feel.

Endless.

I don't even sense my climax until it barrels into me like a freight train. He grips me tighter, riding out his own release.

Spent, he shoves me off of him and throws his arm over my waist. This close, I feel his heart hammering madly in his chest. We're conjoined through sweat-slicked limbs and damp hair. Mine sticks to him, tugged with every move he makes.

He tenses, even before I break the silence.

"Tell me about your family." I'm testing him again.

He hisses at the challenge, his arm flexing over my hips. "I—"

"No," I say before he can reply. "Tell me… Tell me about your sister."

He turns to stone against me, painfully rigid. His arm is a steel beam, weighing me down and the heat from him cools as if snuffed out. "She died," he says, but there's more to it.

More than I know better than to ask for. The strength of his lust is the deciding factor here: Does he really want me so badly?

"And with her, so did my family. My father all but surrendered to the Winthorps after. I would have too, if it weren't for Vanya."

I stiffen. Vanya, who he loves like a father, and a man who may be mine as well.

"Does that bother you?" Mischa wonders. "That you could be his bastard?" He draws me closer, his lips finding my throat.

The intimacy of the embrace sends a shock through me—he knows that. Hell, he taunted me before, throwing my discomfort back in my face: *You don't like to be touched.*

So he touches me, sliding his hands to the front of my belly.

"T-tell me about your father," I counter.

"He went mad when my mother died. And Aljona's death destroyed him." There's no emotion in his voice. He almost sounds too distant. Too detached—a stranger retelling some story he heard once upon a time. "But he grew bitter before the end. He started to resent the *mafiya*. Resent its leaders —Sergei most of all."

"And you?" For a second, I assume he didn't hear me. I'm not even sure where the question came from. Maybe it's something he said before: *I know what it is like to be shunned by your own father.*

"He made his choice," Mischa says—but I cut too deep. His hands readjust in retaliation, sliding down my inner thigh. "And I made mine."

"And…" A grunt rips from me as he traces my outer lips in a series of featherlight touches. I pant, fighting to maintain my train of thought. "What about—"

"Let me ask *you* something. If your perfect husband waltzed into this place and demanded you go back. Would you?"

"I could have left—"

"But what if he had leverage?" Something in his tone makes my stomach churn ominously. "Like your sister. Or…your son?"

"Stop it!" I lunge for the side of the bed, but he tightens his grip, bear-hugging me to his chest. The more I struggle, the harder he grips me. Voice rasping, I choke out, "Why the hell do you like torturing me?"

"I'm *not*."

And that's the worst part. I can hear the pain in his voice as I go limp in his arms. He's hidden it well up until now—but Mischa Stepanov can only control his emotions for so long. And I don't want to think about why he's asking this now. Why, even as I struggle, he doesn't hurt me.

Why he won't let me go.

"I'm not," he repeats gruffly. "So answer the fucking question—"

"No!" I deflate as my voice echoes throughout the room, high-pitched and breathy. "I wouldn't go back. Never—"

"You want to know about me?" he says as if this is some twisted game of tit-for-tat. "My father disowned me. At first, I was too weak. Then too strong. Then too much like *them*." He chuckles darkly. "The Winthorps. My own father hated what I became—the same monster Anna saw. And Aljona. And Vanya…"

Suddenly, he shoves me aside and rises from the mattress. I watch him pace, the muscles in his back rippling with tension. "They were disgusted. They thought I was the corrupted one. But I am still alive, Little Rose." His eyes meet mine, shining with rage and anger and…pain. "I'm still alive. And them? Where are they?"

He storms from the room, leaving the silence to fill in the answer for him.

Where are they?

Gone.

CHAPTER 24

The next morning, I visit the girl. Mouse. One night and she already looks better. Color paints her cheeks, and her eyes are open when I enter her room, tracking my every movement.

"Good morning," I say tentatively.

She blinks, but I notice her hands twitch over the surface of her blanket. She's alert, at least.

"I've brought you something to eat," I add, nodding to the tray I'm holding. Everything on it is courtesy of Vanya: cold porridge, bread, and ice water. "I'll leave it here."

I place the tray on the nightstand beside her bed. As I back away, she sits up and snatches the bread, breaking it in half. Watching her devour each morsel, I can't help but guess just how young she is. Ten maybe? Older?

Her frail, slight frame proclaims stunted growth, but her eyes are too bright for a younger child. Only God knows what she saw before the day Nicolai offered her up as a drug mule.

"Don't eat so fast," someone scolds from the doorway, making me jump. Dressed in gray fatigues, Mischa storms into the room, his arms crossed. "You'll make yourself choke. Are you a girl or a pig?"

He advances toward the bed and snatches the second half of bread from the girl's hand—but rather than flinch from him, she flashes a wicked grin and shoves the remaining bread into her mouth.

"Pig, then," Mischa says in disgust. He reaches out, ruffling the girl's ratty hair. His large palm covers nearly her entire skull, but she doesn't cringe at the contact. "Shame. Pigs can't learn to fight with knives. Not that you'll be getting any more lessons for a while—"

He breaks off and his entire body goes rigid. I must have made a sound. Shock flits across his expression as he spots me in the corner before a cold frown smothers all emotion. His hand leaves Mouse, curling into a fist as he turns for the door.

"Don't." I start after him. Almost against my will, my hand brushes his shoulder. "Stay. I'll go—"

Alarm steals my voice as he snatches my wrist, dragging me into the hall. Shadows obscure the corner he shoves me into. I can only make out the line of his jaw, stern and clenched. Without even seeing his face, I know he's angry. The man radiates rage the way some do their natural scent.

"I want to show you something," he says gruffly. "Tonight."

My mind goes blank. I'd been anticipating a scathing insult. Not a request. "W-what?"

He doesn't answer. Instead, he continues down the hall, leaving me to stare after him. Before descending the steps, he cocks his head, eyeing me from over his shoulder.

"You claimed before that you wanted answers. If you think you can stomach them, then be ready."

He comes for me at midnight, when the rest of the safe house has fallen silent. Dressed in black, he appears at the mouth of my room. Without glancing in my direction, he inclines his head. "Are you ready?"

"Yes." I lurch to my feet and enter the hall.

Without waiting for me to catch up, Mischa descends the stairs. In silence, we exit the house, entering the chill of night.

"Where are we going?" I whisper. Maybe I already know he won't answer—it's the act of defiance that matters. He can't order me around. I'm here because I want to be.

I half expect him to take me to the van—and predictably another far-off location where he makes a shady deal with a strange, imposing man.

My heart skips when he leads me off the path instead.

Amongst looming trees and the scuttling of night creatures, I find myself inching closer to him. Every footfall and sharp sound have me jumping, spotting specters in the dark.

"Here." Suddenly, he comes to a stop in a small clearing. Through gnarled branches, the moon looms above, casting barely enough light to see by. It doesn't help any that Mischa towers like a giant, drenching anything near him in shadow. "You have your questions? Ask them now."

"Why here?" I warily lick my lips. It's the perfect place for him to kill me once and for all, leaving my body where Robert could never find it.

He shrugs. "It's safe. Unless you've changed your mind—"

"Fine." I rack my brain for another question and come up with one easily. "Did I see Briar that night?"

He looks away. "And if you did?"

"Fine!" I turn, feeling blindly through the dark. "If you're not serious—"

"Let's hypothetically say that Briar Winthorp wandered from her brother, who offered to trade her life for yours. Does it matter in the end?"

My chest tightens. Could Robert really be so cruel?

Of course he could.

"Is she alive?"

He eyes me for so long that I assume he won't answer. "I'm not sure, but if he can't trade her, she's only a threat to his power."

I force myself to nod. "Fair enough."

"Any other questions while you're at it?" He's mocking me, but I eagerly take the bait.

"Tell me about my mother."

He shrugs, his expression suddenly distant. "You know most of what I know. She was taken by Sergei Vasilev, starting the war."

He's already told me this part of the tale. I don't know why it's still not enough. Maybe I'll always chase any hint of her I can—secrets and second-hand lies are all of her I'll ever have.

"Why?" I ask.

"Because your husband's father began flexing his muscle. Sergei decided he needed to be put in his place."

"So why continue this stupid feud if it was your *mafiya* who started this?"

"We didn't kill anyone, Rose," he snaps. "The Winthorps played dirty."

"But why keep it going for so long?"

He laughs. "Because it's all we know. Why do lions fight hyenas? It's life."

He makes it sound so damn simple. All of this violence and death. I think of Nikolaus, and Kostas, and Sergei.

Then I laugh brokenly, hating how hopeless I sound. "You're really okay with continuing this for forever?"

"Not forever." He reaches out, ghosting his palm along my cheek. "Just long enough."

I turn away, but my jaw burns in the wake of his touch. "So why keep me?"

"Do I really have to tell you again? What I want?" His hand captures mine, forcing me to face him. "This is what I want."

He doesn't give me the chance to resist. His lips descend over mine, his tongue invading. When I stiffen, his hand sinks into my hair.

"No." He draws back enough to nip my bottom lip between his teeth. "Don't fight it."

It. The way he tastes. How he feels. The longer he kisses me, the more my thoughts dissipate. He's worse than the drug Vanya gave me in the aftermath of my severed finger.

I can overcome an opiate, but not him.

"This," he breathes as my lips part further. "This is what I want. Little Rose, letting down her guard, dropping the act. You're mine." His hands cinch my waist, hungrily yanking me closer.

"S-stop!" Panting, I spring back, swiping at my mouth. Surprisingly, the kiss isn't what has my heart racing. It's a pathetic thought that should be the least of my concern. "I don't want to be your trophy—"

"Good. A trophy has no loyalty. It belongs to whoever snatches it at the end of a battle." His gaze rakes me over and narrows. "I don't want a token prize."

"So then what do you want?"

He throws his head back, exasperated. "Do not play stupid —because you aren't. You are not stupid."

"Maybe I need to hear it from you," I counter, breathless. "So just tell me—"

"Fine." He advances, backing me against a nearby tree. His fingers find my hair again, twisting in the strands of it. "Maybe I just like when you bite back. When you prove you're more than Robert Winthorp's pathetic little wife."

"Or maybe it's *you*," I suggest. "You're tired of being the wolf. I've seen you with Mouse. Even Vanya said—"

"Don't." He tugs sharply on my hair, yanking my head back. "Don't make pretty little assumptions you can't back up. You'll just hurt your delicate sensibilities, Rose—"

"But what if I need to?" It's a question I'm only brave enough to ask now. Not of him, but of myself. "What if I need to believe there's more to you than this?" I swipe my thumb across my scarred cheek and watch him eye the marks as well. "What if I need to believe there's more to you than a monster?"

"And why is that?" he demands, his voice low.

"Because…I don't want to crave a monster."

My cheeks sear at the confession, but it's too late. The words taint the air, spoken aloud, and I'm too exhausted to take them back.

He stiffens, suspicious as always. Narrowed eyes betray his first instinct: fight back. He surges forward, crushing me against moss and bark, and I tense, expecting an assault.

Anything but another kiss, deeper than the first. It's dangerous to let him in, but my body doesn't care. It rails against common sense, letting him invade and claim.

It betrays me in every fucking way.

Suddenly, Mischa pulls back, his gaze darting toward the shadows. "Shit," he hisses.

Dazed, my brain is slow to pick up on his unease. "What's going on?"

"Shh!" He slams his hand over my mouth, his body rigid. He's listening for something.

Or someone.

"Your husband might be more tenacious than I gave him credit for," he snarls into my ear. "We need to move. Now!"

Dirt and brambles crunch underfoot as we race through the dark. His grip on my arm is my only tether to stability, steering me forward.

The farther we go, the more disorienting it is trying to make sense of the swaying branches and uneven terrain.

"Stop!" Suddenly, Mischa drags me behind a tree. "Stay here. I'm going to see if we're being followed." He pulls away, slipping into the darkness.

In his absence, the noise of the forest echoes tenfold. Every scurrying creature and gust of wind is a rustling footstep or intruder.

"It's safe."

I jump as Mischa reappears between two trees and beckons me with a jerk of his chin.

"Come. It seems we have 'company.'"

We return to the house, where a black van is parked in the gravel driveway. For a second, I let my imagination play with the scenario that he finally decided to give up and sell me to Robert.

I'll find him waiting for me in the foyer, his smile smug.

Instead, Sergei Vasilev is there, casting a hulking shadow. "I've had some of my men help secure your perimeter. You're lucky I found your camp when I did," he says. "I had a feeling you wouldn't go far, and I don't mind extending my assistance. In return, I have only one request."

"Of course you do." Mischa's grip on my arm tightens. "And what is that?"

"To talk." He nods toward me. "Alone. One minute, no more."

"And if I refuse?"

Sergei laughs. "Don't be foolish, Mischa. Without my help, Robert Winthorp would already be knocking down your door. My resources have kept him at bay for now. Should I reconsider?"

Mischa grits his teeth. "You—"

"Mischa!" Vanya appears from the end of a nearby hall. "We need to talk."

"Fine, then. A minute, Sergei," Mischa says, pushing past him. "A minute."

"You look well enough," Sergei says in his absence, sweeping his gaze over me. "But you and I both know that any more of this reckless foolishness and you and everyone in this house will wind up dead."

"What do you want?"

"I want you to come with me," he says as if such a thing would be as simple as breathing. "See your ancestral home. Learn your real place."

I rub at my temples. It's surreal having him speak to me like this. There's no affection in his voice. Just desperation.

"Why should I?"

"Could you really keep your son safe here?" he asks. "With Mischa?"

Around me, the room spins and narrows as my mind goes blank. I finally notice something clutched between his fingers that I didn't before: a crisp, square envelope.

"W-What?" My voice shakes, so faint I barely hear it.

"This is proof." He shoves the envelope at me. "Proof that your son is still alive. And that only I can help you rescue him from Robert Winthorp."

~ Continues in I: (One) ~

Hey there!

Thank you so much for reading! If you enjoyed the story, please leave a review and recommend the book to any friend you think would love this twisted world. You'd have my eternal gratitude. Even a short sentence goes a long way!

Then, come join the rest of us dark romance lovers in my Facebook Group where you can get snippets, sneak peeks of upcoming books and even help vote on aspects of future novels.

Come to the dark side:

https://www.facebook.com/groups/lanasbeautifulmonsters/

WANT MORE STUFF TO READ?

Join my newsletter and get a **free book**! Plus, you get to stay updated with any new releases, random giveaways and exclusive sneak peeks!
https://www.lanaskybooks.com/newsletter

Other Novels: https://lanaskybooks.com/

DARK, TWISTED ROMANCE

Join my newsletter and get a **free book**! Plus, you get to stay updated with any new releases, random giveaways and exclusive sneak peeks!

https://www.lanaskybooks.com/newsletter

Lana Sky is a reclusive writer in the United States who spends most of her time daydreaming about complex male characters and parenting her Cockapoo Joey. She writes dark, twisted romance across several genres. Her titles include everything from mafia romance to vampires.

facebook.com/AuthorLanaSky

twitter.com/lanasky101

amazon.com/author/lanasky

pinterest.com/lanasky101

goodreads.com/lanasky

instagram.com/lanasky101

bookbub.com/authors/lana-sky

ALSO BY LANA SKY

For more titles by Lana Sky, please visit:

https://www.lanaskybooks.com

www.ingramcontent.com/pod-product-compliance
Lightning Source LLC
Chambersburg PA
CBHW071742190726
48292CB00003B/845